CROCODILE CREEK: 24-HOUR RESCUE

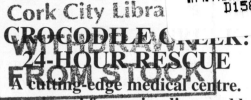

A cutting-edge medical centre.
Fully equipped for saving lives and loves!

Crocodile Creek's state-of-the-art Medical Centre and Rescue Response Unit is home to a team of expertly trained medical professionals. These dedicated men and women face the challenges of life, love and medicine every day!

Two weddings!
Crocodile Creek is playing host to two weddings this year, and love is definitely in the air! But…

A cyclone is brewing!
As a severe weather front moves in, the rescue team are poised for action— this time with some new recruits.

Two missing children!
As the cyclone wreaks its devastation, it soon becomes clear that there are two little ones missing. Now the team has to pull together like never before to find them…before it's too late!

**Marion Lennox's
THEIR LOST-AND-FOUND FAMILY
is the third of four continuing stories
revisiting *Crocodile Creek*. Look out for
the final instalment by Lilian Darcy,
coming next month in Mills & Boon®
Medical™ Romance**

Dear Reader

For the *Crocodile Creek* series I've been working with three wonderful friends: authors Lilian Darcy, Meredith Webber and Alison Roberts. Our stories are based in a tropical paradise, and we've filled our linked hospital and doctors' residence with dedicated—and very sexy—medics from all over the world. Each of these medics has their own romance as the dramas of the wider Crocodile Creek community unfold around them.

In our first series my co-writers introduced the Crocodile Creek obstetrician, a leather-clad, Harley-riding, stiletto-shod redhead, who has sole responsibility for seven-year-old Max. Georgie jumped off the pages as a heroine needing her own story, and my friends gave her to me. They set up a tropical storm like no other, placed Georgie in the middle of it, and said, 'Go for it.'

So I went for it. It needed a truly spectacular hero to get my heroine out of the havoc my fellow writers created. If you love Georgie and Alistair's story then you need to thank my writing mates. They gave me Georgie and my drama. All I've done is lift Alistair out of his very comfortable career as an eminent US neurosurgeon and send him off to Georgie's rescue.

Have fun. I surely did.

Marion Lennox
www.marionlennox.com

THEIR
LOST-AND-FOUND
FAMILY

BY
MARION LENNOX

MILLS & BOON
Pure reading pleasure

First published in Great Britain 2007
Large Print edition 2008
Harlequin Mills & Boon Limited,
Eton House, 18-24 Paradise Road,
Richmond, Surrey TW9 1SR

© Marion Lennox 2007

ISBN: 978 0 263 19951 2

Set in Times Roman 16 on 17¾ pt.
17-0508-56700

Printed and bound in Great Britain
by Antony Rowe Ltd, Chippenham, Wiltshire

Marion Lennox was born on an Australian dairy farm. She moved on—mostly because the cows weren't interested in her stories! Marion writes Medical™ Romance as well as Mills & Boon® Romance. Initially she used different names, so if you're looking for past books search also for author Trisha David. In her non-writing life Marion cares (haphazardly) for her husband, kids, dogs, cats, chickens and anyone else who lines up at her dinner table. She fights her rampant garden (she's losing) and her house dust (she's lost!). She also travels, which she finds seriously addictive. As a teenager Marion was told she'd never get anywhere reading romance. Now romance is the basis of her stories, her stories allow her to travel, and if ever there was one advertisement for following your dream, she'd be it! You can contact Marion at www.marionlennox.com

Recent titles by the same author:

HIS MIRACLE BRIDE*
THE PRINCE'S OUTBACK BRIDE*
THE SURGEON'S FAMILY MIRACLE
RESCUE AT CRADLE LAKE
THE HEIR'S CHOSEN BRIDE
  (Castle at Dolphin Bay)
THE DOCTOR'S PROPOSAL
  (Castle at Dolphin Bay)
HIS SECRET LOVE-CHILD
  (Crocodile Creek)
*Mills & Boon® Romance

PROLOGUE

THE bus trip took a day—thirteen hours with occasional stops for refuelling. All that time Max sat in the far corner of the bus's rear seat, trying to make himself invisible. He stroked Scruffy—Scruffy should be in the cargo hold but the driver had relented—and sang a tiny song into the dog's lopsided ears.

'We're going to Georgie. We're going to Georgie.'

There was another kid on the bus, younger than Max's seven years. He didn't seem to speak, not to the lady he was with or to anyone else. Every now and then, as if drawn, the kid would slip away from the lady and come up to Max's hidey-hole to share in the Scruffy stroking.

'What's your name?' Max asked once, but the kid didn't answer. No matter. It was enough that he was cuddling Scruffy.

Was the kid going to Crocodile Creek, too? Maybe he and the lady he was with knew Georgie.

The lady seemed nice, Max decided. She'd bought Max a sandwich and a drink at the last stop, and an extra sandwich and water for Scruffy. Dad hadn't left him with any money for food. The more Max thought about it, the more he thought he'd been lucky Dad had paid his bus fare.

Maybe he'd had to. Dad was on the run and if Max had been left alone on the streets of Mt Isa, Georgie might have got on her Harley and come and murdered Dad. Georgie's anger was great. She'd never yelled at him, but she'd yelled at Dad. Dad had punched her once and Georgie had punched him right back.

He was going to Georgie.

How much longer?

'Soon we'll be there,' he told Scruffy and the silent kid. 'Soon we'll be with Georgie and she'll punch anyone who's mean to us. If Dad comes and gets us, she'll punch him again.'

But she'd never been able to stop Dad taking him away every time he'd wanted to.

'Dad won't want me any more,' he told his disreputable little dog and his silent friend. 'We'll be safe. Georgie can be our mum.'

The little dog nuzzled into Max's windcheater, infinitely comforting.

'Yeah, Georgie can be your mum, too,' he whispered to the little dog. 'There'll be you and me, and Georgie can be Mum to both of us. She's waiting.'

CHAPTER ONE

'GINA, you can have Alistair Carmichael or you can have me. But not both.'

Gina chuckled.

'I mean it.'

'No, you don't.' Dr Georgie Turner's reputation was that of drama queen—wild girl of Crocodile Creek Hospital. Georgie's favourite party gear consisted of close-fitting leather pants, which showed every curve of her neat, trim body, and low-cut tops displaying an excellent cleavage. Her cropped curls were jet black and shining, and her lips were always glossed dramatic crimson. Her beloved Harley Davidson for normal travel and an off-road bike for the rough stuff completed the picture.

Georgie. Ready for anything.

Georgiana Turner, obstetrician extraordinaire.

Georgie was Gina's best friend. Gina loved her to bits. Underneath that admittedly really brash exterior Georgie had a heart as soft as putty.

'To know you is to love you,' Gina said simply. 'I love you. All your patients love you. Let Alistair know you and he'll love you, too.'

'Right. Like he got to know me last time. He'll use the occasion to lecture me on morals while you guys are signing the register.' Georgie took a deep breath and glowered for added emphasis. 'No. There are some things up with which I will not put.'

Gina sighed. She and Georgie were doctors at Crocodile Creek, base for Air Sea Rescue and the Flying Doctor for most of far north Queensland. Gina was engaged to Cal, another Croc Creek doctor. Six months ago Alistair, Gina's only cousin, had flown in from America to see what sort of set-up his baby cousin was getting herself into.

Unfortunately his visit had coincided with a ghastly patch in Georgie's life. Georgie's stepfather had just dragged her small half-brother away to join him in the seedy life Georgie knew he led. Max was seven years old. Their mother had disappeared into the limbo of drug addiction soon after giving birth to him and Georgie had become Max's surrogate mum. She loved him so fiercely it was as if he was hers.

But he wasn't hers. Half-sisters had fewer rights than fathers, no matter how creepy Georgie's stepfather was. She'd had to let him go.

So Georgie had waved Max off, and then she'd gone to Gina's engagement party. She had been off duty. She'd been trying desperately not to cry. She'd hit the bar, and then Alistair-Stuffed-Shirt Carmichael had asked her to dance.

Which had been…unfortunate.

Alistair had a great body. He was big and warm and strong, and she'd had too much to drink, too fast. She'd seen him earlier in the day and had thought—vaguely—that he was gorgeous. Now, at the party, battered with shock and grief, she'd let her hormones hold sway. She'd let him hold her as she'd needed to be held. She'd flirted unashamedly, and then…

He'd half carried her from the hall and they'd both known what his intentions had been. She hadn't cared. Why the hell should she care when her life was going down the drain?

Only Gina had intercepted them at the door. 'Georgie,' she'd said in that soft voice, the one that said she cared, and suddenly Georgie had pushed away from Alistair, then sat down on the hall steps and sobbed her heart out, while the rest of Crocodile Creek had streamed in and out around her.

'What the hell…?' Alistair had demanded.

And Georgie had looked up at him and said,

through tears, 'I'm sorry, mate. It's not that I don't fancy you. I'm just drunk.'

He'd turned, just like that. From the big, gentle man he'd seemed to the prissy, disapproving toad he really was.

'This is your best friend, Gina?' He'd said it incredulously.

'Yes. She's just—'

'I've just had too much to drink,' Georgie had said, cutting across his question and glaring daggers at Gina, sending visual refusal for Gina to tell him more. 'Gina's right. I gotta go to bed.'

'I'll take you,' Gina had said.

'But it's your engagement party,' Alistair had objected, staring at Georgie as if she'd been some sort of pond scum.

'That's OK,' Gina had said. 'I'll come back soon, but I'm taking my friend home first.'

'You don't need to take me. I have wheels. Hey, you want a ride on my bike?' Georgie had asked, veering off on a tangent and motioning to her beloved Harley parked nearby.

'I think we might leave your bike where it is, don't you?' Gina had said, and had smiled and tugged the decidedly wobbly Georgie to her feet. 'I know you take risks on that thing but we don't want to push it.'

So that had been Georgie's introduction to Alistair. The next day Gina had taken him for a tour of the hospital and he'd been flabbergasted to find Georgie was an obstetrician.

'She's a really good one,' Georgie had heard Gina tell Alistair as they'd disappeared from sight. They'd thought she'd left the ward but she'd forgotten something and returned just in time to hear them talk about her. 'We're lucky to have her.'

'I know you're desperate for doctors,' Alistair had said. 'But I sure as hell wouldn't let her within a mile of any patient of mine.'

So that had been that. Alistair had left the day after, flying back to his very important career as paediatric neurosurgeon in a prestigious US hospital. Georgie had been delighted to see the end of him. But now…

'He's giving you away,' she moaned to Gina. 'We'll have to be in the same church as each other.'

'It's not like he's best man. You won't have to partner him.'

'He thinks I'm a slut.'

'Hey, he was taking you to bed. His behaviour wasn't exactly above reproach.'

'He was taking me to bed because he thought I was a slut.'

'Exactly.'

'So two sets of appalling behaviour cancel each other out?' She flopped onto the bed and groaned theatrically. 'Agh, agh, agh.'

'You could always turn over a new leaf,' Gina said cautiously. 'Greet him in twin set and pearls.'

Georgie choked. 'Yeah. I could.'

'That's what his fiancée wears.'

Georgie lifted her head from the pillows and gazed at Gina in astonishment. 'He has a fiancée?'

'Eloise. He's been engaged for years.'

'So he was engaged when he carted me off the dance floor?'

'See what I mean? Two sets of bad behaviour, and yours is the lesser.'

'Twinset, eh?' Georgie said, and looked thoughtfully at her reflection in the mirror. Her soft black top had crept up a little. She tugged it down to make it more revealing. Which was very revealing.

'Don't you dare,' Gina said nervously. 'Behave.'

'I don't have to wear twinset and pearls as bridesmaid?'

'I was thinking you might like to wear purple tulle.' And then, as Georgie stared at her in horror, Gina giggled and threw a pillow at her friend. 'Gotcha.'

'Cow. Purple tulle?'

'Wear what you want,' Gina said. 'You're my only bridesmaid so the choice is yours. Leathers if you want.'

'Sleek black,' Georgie said, and grinned. 'Not trashy.'

'Trashy if you want.'

'I only do that—'

'I know. When you're angry. But, Georgie…' She hesitated. 'Do you know where Max is now?'

Georgie's smile faded. She picked up the pillow Gina had just tossed at her and hugged it, like it was a baby.

'I have no idea. I had a phone call five months ago, saying he was in Western Australia, but they were moving on that day. My stepfather's always one step in front of the law.'

'Oh, Georg…'

'I wish he'd get caught,' Georgie said fiercely. 'I know he's involved up to his neck in drugs. I want him to go to prison.'

'Because then you'd get Max back?'

'I'm all he's got.'

'Your stepfather must love him to keep him with him.'

'Don't you believe it,' Georgie said fiercely. 'He's just using him. Last time he was here—last time Ron spent time inside—Max told me he does the running. He acts as lookout. Max shops for them when Ron doesn't want to get recognised. Ron even used him for drops. When he was six years old!'

'Oh, Georg…'

'Ron's rotten,' Georgie muttered. 'My whole family's rotten. That's why I'm here in Crocodile Creek—I'm as far as I can get from any of them. Except Max. My one true thing. Max—and I can't do a thing about him.'

There was a long silence. Gina stared at her friend in real concern. Georgie, who'd hauled herself up the hard way, who'd fought her way through medical school, who'd come from the school of hard knocks and was tough on the exterior, but underneath…

'If you really don't want to be my bridesmaid…' she said tentatively, and Georgie's eyes flew up to meet hers.

'Who said I didn't want to be your bridesmaid?'

'But Alistair…'

'I can cope with Alistair Carmichael,' she said grimly. 'He's the least of my worries. Engaged, huh? I can cope with Alistair Carmichael with my hands behind my back.'

'Georgie…'

'Nothing outrageous,' she said, and threw up her hands as if in surrender. 'I agree.'

And then she added, under her breath, 'Or nothing outrageous that you're going to know about.'

It had been some flight. Alistair emerged into the brilliant sunshine of Crocodile Creek feeling almost shell-shocked. He'd been coping with sleepless nights before he'd left. They were setting up a new streamlined process to move patients from Theatre to Intensive Care—not such a difficult process when you said it like that, but in reality, with paediatric problems the transfer was too often a time of drama. He'd orchestrated a whole new method of processing transfers, and he'd hoped to have it securely in place before he'd left, but there'd been last-minute glitches. He'd spent the days before he'd left going through the procedures over and over, supervising mock transfers, timing, making sure the team knew exactly who was doing what.

In the end he'd been satisfied but Eloise had driven him to the airport and even she had been concerned.

'You're pushing yourself too far.'

'Says the youngest ever professor of entomology.'

'I know my limits, Alistair.'

'I know mine, too. I can sleep on the plane.'

But as it had turned out, he hadn't. There'd been turbulence and the plane had been diverted to New Zealand. There he'd endured eight hours in an airport lounge and finally clearance to fly on. More turbulence—this time so severe that some passengers had been injured. Apparently there was a cyclone east of Northern Australia.

Luckily it was southeast of Crocodile Creek and the last short leg had been drama free. Thank God. He descended the plane steps, looking forward to seeing Gina. Trying not to look exhausted. Trying to look as if he was eager for this visit to begin.

Gina wasn't in the small bunch of waiting people. Instead…

His heart sank. Georgie. Dr Georgiana Turner.

He'd hoped she'd have left town by now. What Gina saw in this…tramp, he didn't know.

'Hey, Alistair.' She waved and yelled as he crossed the tarmac.

She was chewing gum. She was wearing tight leather pants and bright red stilettos. She had on a really tight top—so tight it was almost indecent. She was all in black. The only colour about her was the slash of crimson of her lips, her outrageous shoes and two spots of colour on her cheeks.

'How's it going, Al?' she said, and chewed a bit more gum.

'Fine,' he said, trying to be polite and not quite succeeding. 'Where's Gina?'

'See, she was expecting you yesterday. So today she and Cal are running a clinic out on Wallaby Island. The weather's getting up so they thought they ought to go when they could.'

'You couldn't have taken her place?'

'Hey, I deliver babies. Gina's the heart lady. There's not a lot of crossover. You got bags?'

'One. Yes.'

She sniffed, in a way that said real men didn't need baggage. She turned and headed for the baggage hall, her very cute butt wiggling as he walked behind her.

It was some butt.

OK, that's what he couldn't allow himself to think. That was what had landed him into trouble in the first place. She was a tart. Somehow she'd gained a medical degree but, no matter, she was still a tart.

But even so, he shouldn't have tried to pick her up.

Now they stood side by side at the luggage carousel, waiting for his bag. It took for ever. There were other doctors there from the plane.

'There's some other wedding happening here,' he ventured for something to say, and Georgie nodded, looking at the baggage carousel as if it was she who'd recognise his bag.

'Yep. One this Saturday, one next. Planned so those going to both needn't make two trips. We were starting to think there'd be no guests for the first one.'

'It's some storm down south,' he said reflectively. 'That's how I met these guys. The trip from New Zealand should have been cancelled. We hit an air pocket and dropped what felt like a few thousand feet. Anyone who wasn't belted in was injured.'

'You got called on as a doctor?'

'A bit. I was asleep at first.'

'Off duty,' she said blankly, and he winced. There was no criticism in her voice. It was a simple statement of fact, but she knew how to hurt. When he'd woken to discover the chaos he'd felt dreadful. He'd helped, but other doctors had been more proactive than him.

'Look, I—'

'Is this your bag? It must be. Everyone else has theirs.'

'It's mine,' he said, and she strode forward and lugged it off the conveyor belt before he could stop her. She set it up on its wheels and tugged out the handle, then set it before him. Making him feel even more wimpish.

'Right,' she said. 'My wheels are in the car park.'

'Your car?'

'My wheels.' She was striding through the terminal, talking to him over her shoulder. He was struggling to keep up.

He was feeling about six years old.

'Hey, Georg.' People were acknowledging her, waving to her, but she wasn't stopping. She was wearing really high stilettos but still walking at a pace that made him hurry. She looked like something out of a biker magazine. A biker's moll?

Not quite, for her hair was closely cropped and cute—almost classy. The gold hoop earrings actually looked great. She was just…different.

'Doc Turner.' An overweight girl—much more your vision of a biker's moll than Georgie—was yelling to get her attention. 'Georgie!'

Georgie stopped, spinning on her stilettos to see who was calling.

The girl was about eighteen, bottle-blonde, wearing jeans that were a couple of sizes too small for her very chubby figure and a top that didn't cover a stomach that wobbled. She was pushing a pram. A chubby, big-eyed toddler clung to a fistful of her crop top, and a youth came behind, lugging two overstuffed bags. The youth looked about eighteen, too, as skinny as his partner was chubby.

They were obviously friends of Georgie.

'Lola,' Georgie said with evident pleasure. 'Eric. How goes it?'

'Eric's mum's paid for us to go to Hobart,' Lola said with evident pride. 'She's gonna look after us for a coupla weeks till all me bits get back together.'

'Lola had a lovely little girl last week,' Georgie told Alistair, looking into the pram with expected admiration. 'It was a pretty dramatic birth.'

'Had her on the laundry floor,' Lola said proudly. 'Eric had gone to ring the ambos and there she was. Pretty near wet himself when he came back.'

'Lola, Eric, this is Dr Carmichael,' Georgie said. The rest of the passengers from the plane were passing them on the way out to the car park. Nice ordinary people with nice ordinary people meeting them. Not a tattoo in sight.

Lola had six tattoos that he could see. Eric... Eric was just one huge tattoo.

'Doc Carmichael is Gina's surrogate father, here to give her away at the wedding,' Georgie said.

'He's Gina's surrogate father?' Lola checked him out. 'What's surrogate?' Then she shrugged, clearly not interested in extending her education. 'Well, he's older than my old man so I guess he'll do.' She surveyed him critically. 'That silver in your hair. Natural?'

'Um...yes,' Alistair said, discomfited.

'Looks great. Love a bit of silver. Looks real distinguished. Eric, you oughta get some put in. Next time I get me tips done you come, too.' She moved forward a bit to get a closer look and smoothed Alistair's lapel in admiration. 'Cool suit. Real classy. Anyone ever told you we don't do suits in this town?'

'You taking him into town?' Eric asked.

'Yeah,' Georgie said.

'You got a spare helmet?' Lola demanded. 'He's gonna look real dorky in that suit on the back of your bike. And what about his bag?'

'I've got a spare helmet and I hooked up the trailer.'

'Sheesh,' Eric said. 'Rather you than me, mate. She rides like the clappers.'

'I'm not going on a motorbike,' Alistair said, feeling it was time he put his foot down. 'Georgia, I'll get a cab.'

'Ooh, listen to him,' Lola said, admiring. 'Georgia. Is that your real name?'

'Georgiana Marilyn Kimberly Turner,' Georgie said, grinning.

'Sheesh,' said Lola.

'We gotta go,' Eric said, looking ahead at the security gates with a certain amount of trepidation. 'Lola, you sure about the—?'

'The baby stuff,' Lola corrected him, far too fast, and reached over and gave her beloved a wifely cuff. 'Yeah, it's packed. Shut up.'

Georgie chuckled. It was a good chuckle, Alistair thought, low and throaty and real.

'They're in for a rough flight,' he said, watching the little family head off toward Security. By mutual unspoken agreement they stayed watching. Lola picked the baby up out of her pram, handed her to Eric, lifted the pram and dumped the whole thing sideways on the conveyor belt. Then she grabbed all the bags they were carrying and loaded them on top. Bags, bags and more bags.

A security officer from the far end of the hall had strolled down to where they were tugging their gear off the belt. The officer had a beagle hound on a leash.

The beagle walked up to Lola, looked up at her and sat firmly at her feet.

'Hey, great dog,' Lola said, and fished in her nappy bag. 'You want a peanut-butter sandwich?'

'Don't feed the dog, ma'am,' the officer said curtly, and Lola swelled in indignation.

'Why the hell not? He's too skinny.'

'Can we check the contents of the bag you're carrying, please?'

'Sure,' Lola said, amenable. She walked back to the conveyor belt with her nappy bag, lifted it high and emptied it. She put the baby on top for good measure.

'She's carrying the contents of a small house,' Alistair said, awed, and Georgie grinned.

'That's our Lola. She's one of my favourite patients.'

'I can see that,' he said morosely, and she shrugged, starting to walk away.

'Yeah, it's a long way from the keep-yourself-nice brigade I'd imagine you'd prefer to treat. But we need to be flexible up here, mate. Non-judgmental. Doctors like you wouldn't have a chance in this place.'

He bit his lip. She was being deliberately provocative, he thought. Dammit, he wasn't going to react. But…

'About the bike…'

'Yeah?' she said over her shoulder as she headed outside.

'I'll get a cab.'

'Someone's already taken the cab. I saw it drive off.'

'There must be more than one cab.'

'Not today there isn't. It's the northern waters flyfishing meet in Croc Creek. The prize this year is a week in Fiji and every man and his dog is fishing his heart out. And everyone else from the plane left while we were talking to Lola. You're stuck with me.'

They were outside now, trekking through to the far reaches of the car park. To an enormous Harley Davidson with an incongruous little trailer on the back.

'I can usually park at the front,' Georgie said. 'But I had to bring the trailer.' Once again that unspoken assumption that he was a wuss for bringing more than a toothbrush.

'I'd rather not go on the bike,' he said stiffly.

She turned and stared. 'Why not?'

'I don't—'

'Like the feel of the wind in your hair? It's not a toupee, is it?' She kicked off her stilettos and reached into her saddle bag for a pair of trainers that had seen better days. 'Go on. Live danger- ously. I'll even try to stay under the speed limit.'

'I'd rather not.'

'I brought you a helmet. Even the toupee's protected.'

'No.'

There was a moment's silence. Then she shrugged. Before he knew what she was about she'd hauled his suitcase up and tossed it onto her trailer. Then she shoved her helmet over her curls, clipped it tight and climbed astride her bike. The motor was roaring into life before he had time to say a word.

'Fair enough,' she yelled over the noise. 'It's your toupee after all, and maybe I'd worry myself. You can't take too much care of those little critters. I'll drop the case off at the hospital. It's three miles directly north and over the bridge.'

'You can't—'

'See ya,' she yelled, and flicked off the brake.

And she was gone, leaving a cloud of dust and petrol fumes behind her.

'You dumped him.'

'I didn't dump him. I went to collect him and he declined my very kind offer to be my pillion passenger.'

'Georgie, it's hot out there. Stinking hot.' On the end of the phone Gina was starting to sound agitated.

'That's why I couldn't understand why he didn't accept my offer. He's wearing a suit. A gorgeous Italian suit, Gina. With that lovely hair, his height, those gorgeous brogues… Ooh, he looks the real big city specialist. You wouldn't think someone like that would want to walk.'

'He won't have realised… He'll have thought there were taxis.'

'I told him there weren't.'

'Georgie, I want you to go back and get him.'

'No way.'

'In a car. You could have taken a hospital car.'

'What's wrong with my bike?'

'Georgie Turner, are you my very best friend and my bridesmaid or what?'

'I might be,' she said cautiously.

'Then your job as my bridesmaid is to make sure that the man who's going to give me away doesn't turn into a grease spot while hiking into Crocodile Creek.'

'He shouldn't—'

'Georgie.'

'He thinks I'm some species below bedbug.'

'You wore your leathers?'

'So what?'

'And your stilettos?'

'I dressed up. I thought it was important to make a good impression.'

'Georgie, go fetch him.'

'Won't,' Georgie said, but she grinned. OK, she'd made her point. She supposed the toad could be fetched. 'Oh, all right.'

'In the car,' Gina added.

'If I have to.'

'You have to. Tell him Cal and I will be back at dinnertime.'

'Sure,' Georgie said, and grimaced. 'He'll be really relieved to hear that higher civilisation is on its way.'

The kid was sitting in the middle of the bridge. He'd be blocking traffic if there was any traffic, but Crocodile Creek must hunker down for a midday siesta. Alistair hadn't passed so much as a pushbike for the last mile.

He'd abandoned his jacket, slinging it over his shoulder and considering losing it altogether. It was so hot if he'd really been wearing a toupee he'd have left it behind a mile ago. He was thirsty. He was jet-lagged to hell and he was angry.

There was a kid in the middle of the bridge. A little boy.

'Hi,' he said as he approached, but the child didn't respond. He was staring down at the river, his face devoid of expression. It was a dreadful look, Alistair thought. It wasn't bored. It wasn't sad. It was simply…empty.

He was about six years old. Indigenous Australian? Maybe, but mixed with something else.

'Are you OK?' Alistair asked, doing a fast scan of the riverbank, searching for someone who might belong to this waif.

There was no one else in sight. There was no answer.

'Where's Mum or Dad?'

'Dad's fishing,' the child said, breaking his silence to speak in little more than a quavering whisper. Alistair's impression of hopelessness intensified.

'And you're waiting for him to come home?'

'Yeah.'

'Maybe you could wait somewhere cooler,' Alistair suggested. The middle of the bridge was so hot there was shimmer rising from the timbers.

'I'm OK here.'

Alistair hesitated. This kid had dark skin. Maybe he wouldn't burn like Alistair was starting to. If his dad was coming soon…

No. The child was square in the middle of the bridge and his face said he was expecting the wait to be a long one.

He squatted down beside the boy. 'What's your name?'

'I'm not allowed to talk to people I don't know.'

'I'm a doctor,' Alistair said. 'I'm here to visit the doctors at the Crocodile Creek Hospital. I know them all. Dr Gina Lopez. Dr Charles Wetherby. Dr Georgie Turner.'

The kid's eyes flew to meet his.

'Georgie?'

'You know Georgie?'

'She helps my mum.'

'She's a friend of mine,' Alistair said gently, knowing he had to stretch the truth to gain trust. 'She'll be at the hospital now and that's where I'm going. If I take you there, maybe she could take you home on the back of her motorbike.'

The child's eyes fixed on his, unwavering.

'You're a doctor?'

'I am.'

'You fix people?'

'Yes.'

'Will you fix my mum?'

His heart sank. This was getting trickier. The sun was searing the back of his neck. He could feel beads of sweat trickling downward. 'What's wrong with your mother?'

The child's expression had changed to one of wary hope. 'She's sick. She's in bed.'

What was he getting himself into? But he had no choice. 'Can you take me to your mum?'

'Yes,' the little boy said, defeat turning to determination. He climbed to his feet, grabbed Alistair's hand and tugged. 'It's along the river.'

'Right,' Alistair said. He definitely had no choice. 'Let's go.'

CHAPTER TWO

SHE nearly missed him. She drove slowly back toward the airport, starting to feel really guilty. It was unseasonably hot even for here, she thought. The wind was starting to feel like they were in for a major storm, even though the sky was clear.

There was a cyclone out to sea—Cyclone Willie—but it was so far out it should never come near them. The weather guys on the radio were saying the winds they were feeling now were from the edge of the cyclone.

Just don't rain for Mike and Em's wedding tomorrow, she told the weather gods. Or for Gina's the Saturday after.

Right. Back to worrying about Alistair. She'd gone two miles now and was starting to be concerned. Surely he should have walked further than this. But it was so hot. She should never have let her temper hold sway. He wouldn't have realised how hot it was.

Maybe he'd left the road to find some shade. She

slowed down and started studying the verges.
Here was the bridge…

She nearly didn't see them. A path ran by the
river, meandering down to a shanty town further
on. Here were huts built by itinerant fishermen, or
squatters who spent a few months camping here
and then moved on. Periodically the council
cleared them but they came back again and again.

There was a man in the distance, just as the track
disappeared into trees. Holding a child's hand.

Even from this distance she could pick the neat
business suit and jacket slung over his shoulder.
Not Crocodile Creek wear. Alistair.

What the hell was he doing? She pulled onto the
verge and hit the horn. Loudly. Then she climbed
out and waved.

In the distance Alistair paused and turned. And
waved back.

Who was he with?

She stood and waited. He'd have talked one of
the local kids into taking him to shelter, she
thought, expecting him to leave the child and come
back to the road. He didn't. He simply stood there,
holding the child's hand, as if he expected her to
come to him.

Really! It was hot. She was wearing leather
pants. OK, maybe they weren't the most practical

gear in this heat. She'd put them on to make a statement.

She'd also put her stilettos back on before bringing the car out. Her nice sensible trainers were back at the hospital.

He expected her to walk?

He wasn't moving. He simply stood by the river-bank and waited.

Didn't he know you didn't stand near the river? Not for long. There were crocs in this river. It was safe enough to walk on the bank as long as you walked briskly, but to stand in the one spot for a while was asking for trouble.

OK. She gave a mental snort and stalked down the path toward them. Dratted stilettos…

Davy Price.

She recognised the child before she'd reached the riverbank. Immediately her personal dis-comfort was forgotten. What the hell was Alistair doing, holding Davy's hand? Davy was six years old. He was the eldest of four children, the last of whom she'd delivered four days earlier. They lived in the worst of this motley collection of shacks.

While Lizzie, Davy's mum, had been in hospital, she'd tried to persuade her to move to council housing. But…

'My old man wants to live by the river. He won't move.'

Georgie fretted about the family. Lizzie's 'old man' was Smiley, an indolent layabout, drunk more often than not. Lizzie tried desperately to keep the kids healthy but she was almost beaten. To let her go home to this mosquito-ridden slum had gone against every piece of logic Georgie possessed. But you can't make people do what they don't want—who knew that better than Georgie?

But now… She slipped on her way down the grassy verge and she kicked her stilettos off. By the time she reached them she was almost running.

'What's wrong, Davy?' she asked as she reached them. She ignored Alistair for the moment. It'd take something really dire to prise this shy six-year-old from his mum. There had to be something badly amiss. How had Alistair become involved? She had him twigged as the sort of guy who didn't get involved.

He was still holding Davy's hand. He was obviously very involved.

'Mum said to go and get Dad,' Davy whispered. 'But Dad's gone fishing.'

'He went out this morning?'

'He was going to win some prize,' Davy said, and swiped a grimy fist over an even more grimy face. 'But Mum can't get out of bed and the baby keeps crying and crying and there's nothing for Dottie and Megan to eat. I don't know what to do.'

'So Alistair's taking you home,' she said, casting Alistair an almost approving glance before stooping and tugging the little boy close.

'He said he was your friend,' Davy whispered.

'Of course he's my friend.' She hugged the little boy hard and then put him away from her, holding him at arm's length. She glanced up at Alistair and surprised a look of concern on his face. Well, well. The guy had a human side.

'OK, let's go find your mum and see if we can help until your dad comes back,' she said.

'That's just what we were doing,' Alistair said. 'But you're very welcome to join us.'

The hut was one of the most poverty-stricken dwellings Alistair had ever seen. The smell hit him first—an almost unbelievable stench. Then they rounded a stand of palms and reached the hut itself. Consisting of sheets of rusty corrugated iron propped up by stakes with a roof of the same iron weighted down by rocks, it looked more a kid's cubby hut than a real house.

'My God,' he whispered, and Georgie cast him a warning look.

'Most of these houses are better,' she said. 'But they're mostly used by itinerant fishermen, not by full-time residents. Even so... This hut is a long way from any other for a reason. Davy's dad is...not very friendly.'

He was starting to get a clear idea of Davy's dad and it wasn't a flattering picture. What sort of man left a wife who'd just given birth while he joined a fishing competition?

'You don't know the half of it,' Georgie said grimly, watching his face and guessing his thoughts. 'Stay out here for a moment and I'll see what's happening.'

She ducked inside the lean-to shed, leaving him outside, trying to ignore the smell.

Her inspection lasted only seconds. 'Come in,' she called, and something in her voice prepared him for what was inside.

The hut consisted of a rough chimney at one end with a dead fire at the base, a table and an assortment of camping chairs in various stages of disrepair. There were two double-bed mattresses on the floor and that was the extent of the furnishings. There was a baby lying in the middle of one mattress, wrapped neatly enough in a faded blue blanket. On the other bed were two little girls, four and two maybe. They were huddled as closely as they could get to a woman lying in the middle of the bed. The woman looked like she was sleeping. But…

'She's almost unconscious,' Georgie said, stopping his deepest dread before it took hold. 'The pulse is really thready and she's hot as hell. Damn. I need an ambulance. There's no cellphone reception down here but I'm driving the hospital car. It's parked up on the bridge and there's a radio in that. Right. The mum's Lizzie. The little girls are Dottie and Megan—Megan's the littlest—and this is baby Thomas. Take care of them. I'm fetching help.'

She left before he could answer.

Help.

This wasn't exactly familiar territory. He was a neurosurgeon. He was accustomed to a hospital with every facility he could possibly want. He'd reached the stage in his career where he was starting to train younger doctors. He'd almost forgotten this sort of hands-on medicine.

'Is she dead?' Davy whispered, appalled.

'No.' He hauled himself together. He was the doctor in charge.

'She's not.'

Move. Back to basics. Triage. He did a fast check on the baby—asleep but seemingly OK. He loosened the blanket and left him sleeping. Then he crossed to the mattress, stooped and felt the woman's pulse. It was faint and thready. The two little girls were huddled hard against her, big-eyed with terror.

'Davy, I need you to take your sisters onto the other bed while I look after your mother,' he told the little boy. He made to lift the first girl but she sobbed and pulled away from him.

'He's going to make our mum better,' Davy said fiercely. He grabbed her and pulled. 'Dottie, get off. Now.'

'I promise I'm here to help,' Alistair told them, and smiled. One of the little girls—the littlest— had an ugly bruise on her arm. And a burn on her knuckles. He winced. He remembered this pattern of burn mark from his training. Once seen, never forgotten.

'I'm here to help you,' he said softly. 'I promise. Dottie, Megan, will you let me see what's wrong with your mum?'

'He's Georgie's friend,' Davy said stoutly, and it was like he'd given a password. They shifted immediately so he could work. But they watched his every move.

Alistair smiled at them, then turned his attention to their mother. He didn't know how long it would be before help came. With a pulse like this…

The woman's eyelids flickered, just a little.

'Lizzie,' he said softly, and then more urgently, 'Lizzie.'

Her lids lifted, just a fraction.

On a makeshift bench there was a jug of water, none too clean, but he wasn't bothering about hygiene now. The woman had puckered skin, and she was dry and hot to the touch. A severe infection, he thought. The bedclothes around her were clammy, as if she'd been sweating for days.

He poured water into a dirty cup—there were no clean ones—swished it and tossed it out, then refilled the cup. In seconds he was lifting her a little so he was supporting her shoulders and holding the mug to her lips.

She shook her head, so fractionally he might have imagined it.

'Yes,' he said fiercely. 'Lizzie, I'm Dr Georgie's friend. Georgie's gone for help but I'm a doctor, too. You're dangerously dehydrated. You have to drink.'

Nothing.

'Lizzie, drink.'

'Drink, Mum,' Davy said, and Alistair could

have blessed him. The woman's eyes moved past him and found her son.

'You have to do what the doctor says,' Davy quavered. 'He's Georgie's friend. Drink.'

She closed her eyes. He held her mug hard against her lips and tilted.

She took a sip.

'More,' he said, and she took another.

'Great, you're doing great. Come on, Lizzie, this is for Davy.'

He pushed her to drink the whole mug. Sip by tiny sip. She was so close to unconsciousness that it seemed to be taking her an almost super-human effort.

These children were solely dependent on her, Alistair thought grimly. And she was so young. Mid-twenties? Maybe even less. She looked like a kid, a kid who was fighting for her life.

He could help. He poured more water into a bowl, stripped back her bedding and started sponging her. 'Can you help?' he asked Davy. 'We need to get her cool.' As Davy hesitated, Alistair lifted Lizzie's top sheet and ripped. OK, this family looked as if they could ill afford new sheets, but he'd buy them himself if he had to. He handed a handful of linen to each of the children.

'We need to keep your mum wet,' he said. 'We

have to cool her down.' He left the woman's flimsy nightgown on and simply sponged through the fabric.

It was the right thing to do, on all sorts of fronts. It helped Lizzie, but it also gave the children direction. Megan seemed a bit dazed—lethargic? Maybe she was dehydrated as well. But Dottie and Davy started working, wetting their makeshift washcloths, wiping their mum's face, arms, legs, and then starting again. It kept the terror from their faces and he could see by the slight relaxing of the tension on Lizzie's face that it was doing her good. Cooling or not, the fact that there was another adult taking charge must be immeasurably reassuring.

He poured another drink for the little girl— Megan—and tried to persuade her to drink. She drank a little, gave a shy smile and started sponging as well.

Brave kid.

Then, faster than he'd thought possible, Georgie was back. She'd run in her bare feet, and she'd hauled an oversized bag back with her.

'This stuff is always in the hospital car,' she said briefly as his eyes widened. 'Emergency essentials.' When she saw what he'd been doing, she stopped short. 'Fever?'

'I'm guessing way above normal. But she's drunk a whole mug of water.'

'Oh, Lizzie, that's great.'

But Lizzie was no longer with them. She'd slipped back into a sleep that seemed to border on unconsciousness.

No matter. Her pulse was already steadying.

'Great work, kids,' Georgie said, setting her bag down on the floor and hauling it open. 'With workers like you guys, you hardly need me, but now I've brought my bag…let's see if what I have here might help her get better faster.'

They worked as a team. The bag was magnificently equipped. Within minutes they had a drip set up and intravenous antibiotics and rehydration were started. Georgie had lugged an oxygen cylinder with her and they started that as well. Covering all bases.

'Oh, God, if we hadn't come…' Georgie whispered.

It didn't bear thinking about. They both knew just how close to disaster the woman had been.

'Check the baby,' he said. He hadn't had time to give the children more than a cursory check, but while they were setting up the drip Davy had lifted the baby onto his knees and was cuddling his little brother. Davy—all of six years old with the responsibility of this entire family on his shoulders.

'Will you let me see him?' Georgie said softly to Davy, and Davy glanced up at her as if he was still uncertain who to trust. She smiled down at him—a tender smile that Alistair hadn't seen before. Another side of Georgie?

Davy relinquished his bundle and Alistair thought, Yeah, I would too if she smiled at me like that.

Crazy thought. Concentrate on work.

Georgie lifted the bundle into her arms, wrinkling her nose at the stench. She laid the baby on the end of Lizzie's bed, removed his nappy and started cleaning.

Was this the sort of thing doctors did here? Alistair wondered. Medicine at its most basic.

'Has Thomas been drinking?' she was asking Davy.

'I dripped water into his mouth when he cried.'

'Good boy,' Georgie said in a voice that was suddenly unsteady. 'You've done magnificently, Davy.' She glanced across at Alistair. 'I'll leave the nappy off. He's hot as well, and probably dehydrated, like his mum. We need a drip here, too, I reckon.'

Alistair checked the bag, and found what he needed. He swabbed the tiny arm, preparing to insert a drip.

'You can do this on newborns?' Georgie

queried. Veins in neonates were notoriously difficult to find.

'I'm a neurosurgeon,' he told her. 'Paediatrics is
my specialty.'

'We don't want brain surgery here,' she whispered. 'We just need the ability to find a vein.'

Which he did. The syringe slid home with ease and
he sensed rather than saw the tension leave Georgie.

She cared about these people, he thought with
something akin to shock. He wouldn't have
thought it of her. But, then, she was an obstetrician. She just hadn't acted like one the first time
he'd met her.

There was the sound of a siren, from far away
but moving closer.

'Davy, can you go up to the road and show them
where to come?' Georgie asked, but as Davy rose
Alistair gripped his hand and held it.

'I'll come with you,' he said. 'Dr Georgie has
done everything we need to do here. Davy, your
mum's going to be OK, and so is the baby. You
found help. You've done everything right.'

The little boy's eyes filled with tears.

'Go and get the ambulance officers with Dr
Alistair,' Georgie said to him. 'And that's the last
thing we'll to ask you to do. We're taking you all
to hospital where we can give you all a great big

meal, pop you all into a lovely comfy bed near your mum and let you all have a long sleep until your mum is better.'

There was one last complication. They wouldn't all fit into the ambulance.

Megan was definitely dehydrated. Thomas hadn't been fed properly, maybe for twenty-four hours. He needed a humidicrib and intensive care. And Lizzie was waking a little more now, emerging from her semi-conscious state but moving to uncomprehending panic.

She was gripping Georgie's hand as if it was her lifeline. Every time she opened her eyes she searched in panic for Georgie. So Georgie had to go with her. Which made four in the ambulance. Lizzie, Megan, Thomas and Georgie.

'I can't go to hospital,' Lizzie murmured as the ambulance officers shifted her to a stretcher. 'Smiley'll kill me.'

'Yeah, well, maybe I'll kill him first,' Georgie said fiercely. 'So it should be quite a battle. Lizzie, you're moving out of here. I told you last time and now I'm insisting. And you needn't be afraid of Smiley. If you agree, I'll swing it so he never comes near you again. We'll organise you safe housing. I swear I'll fix it.'

Alistair blinked. These weren't calming, reassuring words to a desperately ill woman. But it seemed to work. Lizzie slumped back onto the stretcher and the tension seeped out of her.

'You're one of us,' she whispered. 'Thank God. Oh, Georgie, thank God.'

'Right to go?' the senior ambulance officer asked. These two may be ambulance officers but they didn't look like ambulance officers. They looked like fishermen.

'I stopped you fishing,' Lizzie whispered, becoming more aware of her surroundings.

'Nah,' the man said. 'The competition got called off half an hour ago 'cos the wind's getting up. Phyllis Dunn won. She wins every bloody year. Mind, she always ends up raffling her prize in aid of the hospital. Going to Fiji isn't Phyllis's style.'

What sort of town was this, where the ambulance officers went fishing while they were on duty? Alistair wondered. The younger officer looked at Alistair and grinned, guessing his thoughts.

'Hey, you needn't worry, mate,' he said. 'We had the ambulance parked right behind us while we were fishing, and most dramas were going to happen on the river anyway. Right?' he queried his partner, and they lifted the stretcher. They'd have to carry it—there was no car access here.'

'I'm coming with you,' Georgie said. She was cradling the baby in one arm and cuddling tiny Megan in the other.

'Let me carry them,' Alistair said, but as Megan buried her face in Georgie's neck, Georgie shook her head. She gave a rueful smile. 'Megan knows me,' she said. 'And Lizzie trusts me. It's easier if I sweat a bit. But we need Dottie and Davy to go with you. Davy, you know that Dr Carmichael is my friend?'

Davy knew what was coming. He gulped but then he looked up at Alistair and what he read in his face seemed to satisfy him. 'Y-yeah.'

'I want you to help Dr Carmichael drive my car,' Georgie said. 'He's an American and they don't even know what side of the road to drive on. And, Davy, I want you to hold Dottie's hand and take her with you. Will you do that? Dottie, will you do that? We won't all fit in the ambulance and Dr Carmichael will bring you straight to the hospital to be with your mum.'

There was a moment's hesitation.

'It's OK,' Davy whispered to Dottie, and once more he repeated his mantra. 'He's Georgie's friend.'

Dottie stared up at him dubiously, but then seemed to come to a decision. She tucked her hand into Alistair's and held on.

'The key's in my pocket,' Georgie said.

Really? In her pocket? There was a distracting thought coming from left field. He wouldn't have thought there was room for anything at all in those tight-fitting leathers.

She had no hand free to get them out. And he had one hand free.

'Front left,' she said patiently.

Front left. Right. Surgical removal of car keys. But, hell, those pants were tight. Hell, those pants were…

Maybe he'd better concentrate on other things. Dottie was holding his hand, waiting for him to get on with it. The younger ambo officer was looking at him and grinning, and he just knew what the guy was thinking.

What the hell. He grinned back and retrieved the keys, almost managing to keep his thoughts on the job at hand. Almost.

But as the keys came free he had room for another thought. What Georgie had said.

'Australians drive on the left.'

'We do,' Georgie said patiently. 'Problem?'

'You want me to drive Davy and Dottie to the hospital in your car?'

'In the hospital car. That's the idea, Einstein.' She was back to being tough. Any minute she'd start with the gum chewing again. The ambo boys were looking at her in surprise but he didn't have time to think about why she was being like she was.

'Look, this'll be the first time I've driven on the left… I'm not covered. Insurance-wise, I mean. If anything happens to the kids…'

'Here we go,' Georgie said, and sighed. 'American insurance paranoia.' The ambos had already started carrying the stretcher to the door and she was moving with them. 'Firstly, there's no one around to crash into,' she said over her shoulder. 'It's midday, and only mad dogs and Englishmen go out in the midday sun. Or Yankee neurosurgeons. So the roads will be deserted and there's no one to hit. Second, it's a straight line from here to the hospital. You can follow the ambulance. If you're nervous then move over and tell Davy to drive. He's probably as competent as you are.'

And with that she left, leaving him to follow.

The hospital was just as he remembered it. Long and low and cool, open to the ocean breeze. Actually, the ocean breeze was more than a breeze at the moment. The surrounding palms were tossing wildly, and the sea was covered in whitecaps. But the place still looked lovely. If you had to be sick this was one of the best places in the world to be.

Alistair pulled up in the car park and took the two children inside.

The children hadn't complained as their mother had left. Now they took a hand apiece, infinitely trusting. He felt really off balance, walking into Crocodile Creek Hospital Emergency with a child on each hand.

The ambulance was in the unloading bay, already unloaded. He hadn't followed it closely, preferring to travel slowly and safely. For all Georgie's reassurance, the left-hand-drive thing was a challenge, and having two small passengers made him careful.

There was no sign of Lizzie or Megan, but Georgie was in the emergency department, carrying Thomas. She was still in bare feet. He'd picked up her abandoned stilettos from the pathway—they were still in the car—a monument to stupidity. But she didn't look stupid now.

There was a nurse beside her. He recognised this woman from his last visit, too. Grace?

Grace gave him a smile of welcome but Georgie ignored him, bending down to greet the kids.

'Dottie. Davy. Dr Alistair got you here safely,

then? That's great. Well done, both of you. And well done, Davy, for getting help so fast. Now, we're just giving your mum a proper wash and getting her really cool. She hasn't been drinking—that's why she's been sick. You know we popped a needle into her arm, and into Thomas's, to get water in faster? We've done the same to Megan. Megan's having a little sleep. But you guys will be thirsty as well, and probably hungry. So do you want to come and find your mum and Megan straight away or can Grace take you to the kitchen and give you some chocolate ice cream?'

It was exactly the right thing to say, Alistair thought. By the look of that hut, these kids must be starving. But Georgie wasn't sending them away with Grace without their consent. They were being given the choice. Your mum is safe. You can see her now, or there's ice cream on offer. The choice is yours.

'How about you have the ice cream and then come back and see your mum?' Grace said, tipping the scales. 'You know Mrs Grubb, don't you? She gave you ice cream when your mum was having the baby. She's in the kitchen right now, getting out bowls. And I think she has lemonade, too.'

'I really like ice cream,' Dottie whispered, and

she even smiled. It was a great little smile, the first Alistair had seen from the children. He released their hands and watched them go, but as he did so he was aware of a sharp stab of something that almost seemed like…loss? Which was crazy.

The door through to the hospital kitchens swung closed behind them, and he became aware that Georgie was watching him. She had the saline drip looped over her shoulder, holding Thomas low so it was gravity feeding. She needed a drip stand.

'Do you want help with Thomas?' he asked.

'I'll take him through to the nursery in a minute, but apart from horrible nappy rash he seems OK. You know Davy's been dripping water into his mouth? What a hero.'

'He is,' Alistair said, and he thought back to the frail child sitting in the middle of the bridge and felt stunned. Awed.

'You remember Charles Wetherby—our director? Charles has Lizzie in his charge,' Georgie continued. She'd walked over to a drip stand and he moved with her, taking the saline bag from her shoulder and hanging it on its wheeled hook. 'It looks like severe infection. Charles is continuing the IV antibiotics and the nurses are cleaning her up. She's a mess.'

'When did she have the baby?'

'Four days ago.'

The image of Davy was still in the forefront of his mind. Lizzie, going home to the care of a six-year-old. 'You let her go home to that?' he demanded incredulously. 'Did you know her circumstances?'

It wasn't implied criticism. It was a direct attack.

Back home Alistair was head of a specialist neurosurgery unit. He had hiring and firing capabilities and he used them. The voice he had used then was the one that had any single subordinate—and many who weren't subordinate—shaking in their shoes. At least cringing a little.

Georgie didn't cringe. She met his gaze directly, as if she had nothing to search her conscience over.

'Yes.'

'What were you thinking?'

'I wasn't thinking anything. I was making the best of a bad situation. I spent the whole of Lizzie's pregnancy convincing her to come to the hospital for the birth. She's had the last three children at home. But this time I succeeded. She came in. I was hugely relieved, but when her partner insisted she go straight home I sent her with everything she needed. Including a course of antibiotics. No, at that stage she didn't need it, but I knew the hut.'

'It was criminal to let her go back there. You know the little girl's been burned. That's a cigarette burn.'

'I know. That's new. Up until now Lizzie would have stood up to him if he'd hurt the children. It's a sign of how sick she is.'

'But you let her go back.'

'You think I should have chained her up?'

'Surely a woman with sense—'

'Lizzie is a woman of sense,' she said, practically spitting. 'She's had a lousy childhood, she has a dreadful self-image and her partner...'

She broke off. Someone was coming into Emergency—no, two men, a uniformed police officer with a younger man in front of him. The young man was dark, but not the dark of the Australian indigenous people, as Lizzie was. He looked European. Mediterranean? He was dressed in filthy fishing clothes, he looked as if he hadn't shaved for a week, and the smell of him reached them before he did.

He didn't look like he wanted to be there, but the policeman was behind him, prodding him forward, giving him no choice. 'Hi, Georgie,' he said, but he didn't smile. 'You wanted to talk to Smiley?'

'Smiley,' Georgie said, and Alistair stared.

Georgie was tiny, five feet two in her bare feet. She looked like you could pick her up and put her wherever you wanted. Not with that tongue, though. What she unleashed on the man before her was pure ice.

'Thanks, Harry,' she said, and nodded to the policeman with what was to be the last of her pleasantries. 'Alistair, can you take Thomas for a minute?' Before he could answer she'd handed over the sleeping baby, forcing Alistair to move closer to the drip stand. Then she poked her finger into the middle of Smiley's chest and pushed him backward.

'What the hell did you do with Lizzie's antibiotics?' she demanded, and although she spoke softly her words were razors. 'And the supplies we gave her. The nappies. The canned food.'

'I…'

'You sold them, didn't you?' she snarled. 'I don't even have to guess. I know. You took them down to the pub because someone might give you a buck for them. You thieving, filthy piece of pond scum. You nearly killed Lizzie. If Alistair here hadn't found her today, she'd be dead. She'd be dead because you stole her medicine. There's no food in your house. The kids are starving. You spent today on the river and Harry's just pulled you out of the pub. And Megan's bruised arm and burned hand…You did that, didn't you? You stinking, bottom-feeding low-life.'

'Hey—'

'Enough,' Georgie snarled. 'That's enough. Lizzie's conscious—only just, but she's conscious enough to agree to press charges. You stole her medicines and you hit your kids and you burned Megan.'

'I didn't hit anyone. If she says I did then she's lying. And can I help it if the kid plays with matches? I didn't touch her.' The man's reply was scornfully vituperative.

'Oh, yes, you did.' Georgie was still prodding the man in the chest, poking with her finger to emphasise every word. The policeman appeared watchful but he was standing back, letting Georgie have her say.

Alistair was stuck by the drip attached to the baby in his arms. He didn't like this. The man looked…evil?

Georgie obviously thought he was. 'You hit Lizzie all the time, don't you, Smiley? You keep her starving. You thump her around and when she's not looking, you thump your kids. You're nothing but a cowardly—'

'There's no way she'll press charges.'

'Because you'll hit her again if she does? Of course you will. But you never hit anyone bigger than you, do you, Smiley? You're a snivelling coward.'

'Shut up, bitch,' he snarled, but she wouldn't shut up. It was as if she was driving him.

'So what happened on the river today, Smiley?' she spat, continuing to prod him. 'Did you catch any fish? Or did you come last as usual? You play the big man but you're nothing but a loser. The whole town thinks you're a loser and the only way you can big-note yourself is to hit women and kids.'

'Georg,' Harry said urgently, and the policeman took a step forward. So did Alistair but he was holding Thomas, and Thomas was attached to the drip.

'Don't push me,' Smiley yelled.

She pushed him. Hard.

No, Alistair thought. He moved—but he was caught by the drip stand.

'Georg, no,' Harry yelled, and lunged forward.

He was too late.

Smiley hit her. Just like that, Smiley's fist came up and smashed into the side of her face with a sickening crunch. Georgie fell sideways. She'd barely hit the floor before Harry had Smiley, hauling him away, and Alistair was just as fast. In one swift movement he'd hauled the drip stand over so it was lying on the floor and baby Thomas was lying safely beside it. Alistair had Smiley's arms, tugging them behind him. Smiley struggled but he was no match for the two of them.

Georgie lay prone for a moment, but before they could reach her she'd staggered upright, her hand to her cheek, clutching the trolley for support.

They had him secured. Harry was clipping handcuffs on Smiley's wrists, but Alistair was no longer with him. He'd moved to Georgie's side to see the damage. He felt sick. Oh, God, why hadn't he stopped it? Why had she pushed him? She had her hand to her eyes. 'Georgie…'

'He hit me,' she muttered.

'Let me see.'

'No.' She sounded close to tears. Where a moment ago she had been a tight knot of pure aggression, she now sounded limp and defeated. 'He hit me,' she whispered.

'What's he done?' Harry sounded anxious.

'I'll need X-rays,' she whispered, and Harry's face darkened as he turned back to the man he held.

'Smiley Price, I'm arresting you for assault,' Harry said. 'You do not have to say anything but anything you say may be—'

'I know my rights,' Smiley yelled. 'This is a set-up.

'I didn't see a set-up,' Harry said grimly. 'I

saw you assaulting a doctor when she was dis-
cussing your wife's medical treatment.' He
glanced across at Georgie. 'Georg, let Alistair
see your face.'

'Take care of Thomas,' Georgie whispered to
Alistair. On the floor Thomas was considering his
options. He'd been unceremoniously dumped.
Until how he'd been silent, sleeping, mostly
because he was badly dehydrated. But fluid had
been flowing for maybe an hour now and he was
starting to feel more like expressing himself.

He did. He opened his mouth and he roared.

'That's great,' Georgie said, giving a weak
smile. 'Alistair, pick him up.'

He didn't. He took Georgie's hand and tugged
it away from her face.

The punch hadn't hit her eye, for which he was
profoundly thankful. Instead, it had smashed into
her cheekbone. The soft tissue was swelling while
he watched, and the skin had split a little. A trickle
of blood was inching down toward her neck.

'You bastard,' Harry said, twisting Smiley's arm
and dragging him toward the door. He nodded to
Alistair. 'I'll need a witness statement from you.
Get photographs. Not that we'll need them.' He
was gripping Smiley's arm in a hold that said he
wasn't going anywhere. 'If you remember, mate,

you're already on a two-year suspended sentence for theft. With what you've done today they'll throw away the key.'

'Get him out of my sight,' Georgie whispered, as Harry prodded him through the door, and then she roused. 'And if I can find anything at all to charge you with, I will,' she yelled after him. 'Two years is just the beginning.'

The door closed after them.

They were left alone. Except for one screaming baby.

Georgie picked Thomas up before Alistair could stop her. She hugged him tight. The baby's sobs stopped, just like that. Alistair lifted the drip stand and turned back to her. She was hugging the baby as if it was she who needed comfort.

Involuntarily his hands came out to take her shoulders. It was an instinctive gesture of comfort but she drew back as if his touch burned.

'No.'

'I'm sorry…'

'No.' She held her spare hand to her eyes for a moment as if things were more than she could face. Then she took a deep breath and another.

'OK,' she said, moving on. 'Your bag's over in the doctors' quarters. You have the same room as you had last time you were here. Gina will be home about five. There's food and drink in the kitchen. Have a swim. Make yourself at home.'

'Your face needs attention.'

'I'll give it a wash later.' She took a deep breath and tried to smile. 'But wasn't it fantastic? He's been hitting Lizzie and the kids for years and she won't press charges. She's said she will now, and she might when she knows he's going to jail anyway, but it's no longer up to her. I'll be doing the pressing of charges.'

'You planned it,' he said, stunned.

'I knew about the suspended sentence,' she admitted.

'Are you mad? He could have blinded you.'

'He didn't. I've learned how to take a hit over the years. I was moving away as he struck. But I had to let him make contact.'

'You're crazy.'

'And Smiley's in jail. A good afternoon's work, I reckon. Now…I need to sort out a carer for the kids. I need to contact welfare officers and the housing people. I'm moving so fast here Smiley won't know what's hit him. If you can—'

'You let him hit you.'

'Get over it.'

'Of all the…' Before she could stop him he'd lifted Thomas from her arms. He tugged the drip stand with him over to an examination trolley. Gently he laid the little one down. Thomas accepted the move with equanimity. Strange things were happening in his world, and he was learning early that fussing didn't necessarily get him anywhere.

'I don't want him down,' Georgie said, moving to pick him up again, but Alistair intercepted her.

'I've done the triage, Dr Turner. Not before I've checked that eye.'

'It's fine.'

For answer he picked her up and sat her on the trolley next to Thomas. She opened her mouth to squeak a protest but he was already gently probing, checking bone structure, peering intently at her eye, looking for internal bleeding.

She was so slight. A diminutive woman with courage that would put men twice her size to shame. She submitted to his ministrations but he had the feeling she was simply humouring him.

'No brain injury,' she said, gently mocking. 'Nothing here you're interested in.'

Maybe not. But he was suddenly aware of what he'd felt six months ago. The feeling that had surfaced as he'd danced with her.

He'd thought she was a woman with morals somewhere below that of a guttersnipe.

Maybe he'd misjudged her…

'What's happening?'

It was Grace, bursting in to see what was happening. Appalled. 'Georgie, you're hurt. I just saw Harry taking Smiley away. He said—'

'I'm fine,' Georgie said.

'But Harry said Smiley hit you.' Grace sounded incredulous. 'You let him hit you?'

'I had to.'

'She does karate,' Grace said to Alistair. 'She's black belt. No man can get near her. Harry knew that or he'd never…' She'd moved closer to Georgie as she'd spoken, edging in on Alistair's space. 'Harry's feeling dreadful and sent me to check. Let me see.'

'I'm fine.'

'You're shaking.'

'I am not. Leave me be.' Georgie jumped down from the trolley before Alistair could stop her. 'If you want to be useful, take Thomas.'

'That's another reason I'm here,' Grace admitted. 'Lizzie's asking for him and Charles wants to check him. But, Georgie, come through and let Charles see the damage.'

'I'm fine,' Georgie snapped again.

'I'll take care of it,' Alistair said, and Grace looked at him dubiously. Then her face cleared as she obviously remembered stuff she'd been told about him. 'Of course. You're Gina's Alistair. You're a neurosurgeon.'

'That's right,'

'Then I guess you can cope. If you think she needs an X-ray, give a yell.'

'He won't do any medicine,' Georgie said, sounding contemptuous. 'I know US doctors. They think treating people messes with their insurance.'

'Now, that,' Grace said roundly, 'is just plain rude. And wrong. The ambo boys said Alistair's already put in a drip. And I'm sure he'll help any way he can. Won't you, Alistair?'

'Of course.' Black belt in karate, huh? He eyed Georgie with increasing respect.

'I only pick on people my own size,' Georgie said.

'I wasn't thinking—'

'Yeah, you were. Wimp.'

'Georgie, behave,' Grace said severely. Thomas opened his mouth again, a preliminary to wailing. Ready, set, yell. She smiled ruefully down at him. 'OK, sweetheart, I'll take you to your mum. Alistair, there's a digital camera in the desk drawer. Use it. Please. Harry says we need photographs. I'm sorry to leave you like this but this place has gone crazy. I'll be back as soon as I can. Georgie, behave,' she repeated.

And she was gone.

CHAPTER THREE

THERE was a moment's silence. Georgie's hand had crept to her cheek again, hiding the damage.

'I do need to clean and dress it,' he said gently, but she shook her head and started following Grace.

She was limping.

'Georgie?'

'I'm fine.'

'You're not.'

Alistair moved then, fast, catching her by the shoulders and turning her around. Gently. Aware of her black belt.

But her black belt had been punched right out of her.

'Leave me be.' She sounded suddenly…drained.

'Let me see your face. And your foot.'

'No.'

She was like a little wildcat, he thought. Tough as nails, all claws and hiss. But she was shaking. He could feel the tremors in her shoulders.

To hell with the black belt. He lifted her up again and dumped her on the nearest examination trolley. 'Stay where you're put.'

'Do you mind?' She seemed practically speechless. 'I need to—'

'Nothing's more urgent than your face. You should have stayed put in the first place.' He pulled her fingers away. 'Hell, Georgie…'

'Don't swear. You make me feel like it's worse than it is.'

'It's bad.'

'It's not. I've learned how to ride a punch. I can feel my cheekbone. He didn't break anything.'

She'd learned how to ride a punch? In karate? He didn't think so. Everything about this woman spoke of a tough background.

Except that she was an obstetrician.

First things first. If she'd gone to this much effort, it wasn't about to be wasted for want of effort on his part. He wheeled across to the desk by the door and found the camera. 'Let's do this before we do any cleaning.'

'Oh, very good,' she said, and managed a smile. 'OK, I submit.'

'Lie down.'

'No, I—'

'You'll look more pallid and wan against the pillows.'

'I don't want to look like a victim.'

'I'm very sure you do.' He fiddled with the camera. 'If you could manage a few tears…'

She thought about that, and then she managed a smile. It was a great smile, despite the bruising. Like the sun had just come out.

'Right,' she said, and she lay back on the pillows, moving into her role of victim with gusto. He adjusted the camera, turned to focus on her cheek—and to his astonishment her eyes were brimming.

He stared.

'Neat trick, huh?' she said. 'Don't interrupt. I'm thinking sad thoughts.'

Sad thoughts. He couldn't make her out. He focused and shot. The photograph would be damning, he thought. Her dark curls accentuated the pallor of her skin. The knuckle marks of Smiley's hand were clearly visible and the splitting of the skin before it was cleaned looked worse than it actually was.

And she was playing it for all it was worth. Her eyes were brimming, seemingly pain-filled. There were tears coursing down her cheeks.

He wanted to… He wanted to…

'Enough,' she declared as the camera clicked for the fourth time. She swung herself upright.

He put the camera aside and pushed her down again.

'Do you mind?'

'Not at all. Let's do a bit more triage. Foot first.' He'd moved before she knew what he intended. He had her left foot in his hand, lifting it high. 'Ouch.'

'It's fine,' she snapped. 'I can't use that against Smiley.'

'It'd be good if we could,' he agreed, examining her heel with care. 'Hell, woman, were you out of your mind, running in bare feet?'

'I scarcely had a choice.'

'You had a choice as to what to put on this morning.' He hauled a nearby trolley closer and stared dubiously at its contents. 'Stilettos?'

'You're criticising my footwear?'

'I am. There's a splinter in here. A deep one.'

'I'll get it out myself.'

'Shut up and lie back,' he told her, and then, as she struggled to sit up and opened her mouth to argue, he took her by the shoulders and propelled her back onto the pillows. 'Not a word.'

'You're not an emergency doctor,' she said resentfully, and he tugged on gloves, located a pile of antiseptic swabs and ripped one open.

'No. I'm a neurosurgeon. You want a little brain surgery on the side?'

'Look, honest—'

'Lie still and think of England,' he told her. 'This might sting.'

It did sting. But for a big man he had really gentle hands, she thought as she did what she was told and lay back and thought…well, not of England but of what this man represented.

He'd almost taken her to bed. Six months ago she'd been out of her mind with grief and worry, and Alistair had taken advantage of it.

He hadn't known she'd been out of her mind with grief and worry. Maybe he'd thought she was always a tart.

Well, he was hardly stain-free. Propositioning her when he'd been engaged to another woman…

Was he still engaged? Maybe he was married. She hadn't asked Gina.

What was she doing, wondering what his marital status was? He was a stuffed shirt. An eminent US neurosurgeon. He was about as far from her world as it was possible to get.

'Ouch!' Her exclamation was involuntary. Alistair had positioned the light directly above her foot and was operating with a scalpel and a pair of tweezers. She glanced down at what he was doing and winced.

'A scalpel! You don't think that's a bit of overkill?'

'I promise I'm not amputating.'

'Oh, very good. I'm reassured, I don't think. Yike!'

'I'm sorry, but I'm being quick. Local anaesthetics in the heel will hurt a lot more than I need to hurt you now. So stay still.'

'But a scalpel?'

'If you wiggle, I might be forced to amputate.'

'I want a second opinion.'

He grinned. Which took her aback somewhat. It was a really great grin.

She'd never seen him smile, she thought. Or maybe she had that night six months ago but she'd hardly been in a state where she could remember anything.

She could remember that she'd decided to sleep with him. So there must have been something…

'Got it,' he said in satisfaction, and then, as she made to sit up, he lifted both feet, which had the effect of propelling her down again.

'There's cleaning yet to be done.'

'Fussy…'

'Yeah, and I don't wear stilettos either. But I'm still a qualified doctor.'

He was…gorgeous? Just like last time.

No matter. There was no way she intended to be attracted by this man again. She'd made a fool of herself six months ago and that was the end of it.

She lay back and concentrated on not concentrating on anything at all for a bit. Finally he adjusted a neat dressing on her foot and moved to her end of the bed.

'Now, let's see to your face,' he said. 'Your foot's OK. Just don't walk on it for a bit. It'll bleed.'

'Then your dressing's not good enough.'

'Georgie…'

'I know.' She sighed and glowered, and then submitted as he cleaned her face. He was so gentle. He'd hurt her a bit, getting the splinter out—that had been unavoidable—but he wasn't hurting her now.

'Steristrips will do it,' he said as he worked. 'It doesn't need stitching. But the bruise is extensive. We'll take an X-ray to make sure.'

'I don't need an X-ray. There's nothing displaced. Even if there's a hairline fracture, there's nothing to be done about it.'

'But think of the damage you could do with a broken bone,' he coaxed. 'It's bound to put another year or so on the sentence.'

She stared up at him. And then she choked on an unexpected bubble of laughter.

'That's better,' he said, and smiled down at her, and suddenly they were smiling into each other's eyes like...

Fools?

'I need to put a dressing on,' he said unevenly, and she gave a shaky little nod.

'Yes.'

What the hell was happening? Why did this man have the power to move her?

Hell, hadn't he caused enough trouble in her life?

'Georg!' For some reason—or maybe she knew the reason but she wasn't all that happy to admit it—she hadn't heard the doors opening behind them. Now Alistair turned with what seemed almost a guilty start. Which was crazy. He'd just been...

Looking?

No. He'd been examining a patient. Nothing more. She dragged her eyes away from his face and turned to see who'd entered.

It was Gina—Dr Gina Lopez—walking swiftly into the room and across to Georgie's trolley. She looked frightened. 'I just met Harry,' she said, ignoring Alistair for the moment and concentrating on Georgie. 'He said you made Smiley hit you.'

'I did no such thing.'

She bent to hug her. 'You dope.'

'He'll get put away for ages,' Georgie said, but suddenly her voice was trembling again. 'Gina, don't hug me.'

'She doesn't let people hug her,' Gina told Alistair, pulling back and sounding emotional. She swallowed and turned to her cousin. 'Hi,' she said, and she gave Alistair the hug she'd certainly wanted to give Georgie. 'It's lovely to see you. I'm so sorry Cal and I weren't here to meet you. In the end we couldn't get all our work done on the island anyway—the pilot started to get concerned about the weather and brought us back early. But I gather you've arrived to excitement.'

'You asked Georgie to meet me. Of course I arrived to excitement.'

'She's not always…' Gina paused, turned to her friend sitting up defiantly on the examination trolley, barefoot, leather-clad, dressings on her foot and on her face, her lipstick still defiantly crimson… 'Yeah, OK, she is always exciting,' Gina said. 'But we love her anyway.'

Alistair was starting to look confused. As if he wasn't quite understanding what was going on. Good, Georgie thought, because that was how she was feeling.

'Don't let her stand on her foot,' he managed.

'I'll take her over to the doctors' house,' Gina told him, looking around. She located what she was looking for, darted over and hauled back a wheelchair. 'Can you help her into this, please, Alistair?'

'I'm not getting in that thing,' Georgie said, revolted.

'I want you off that foot for a few hours,' Alistair said. 'Pressure will make it bleed. I also want an X-ray. Get into the chair and we'll take you.'

'Do what the doctor says,' Gina said, and grinned.

'No way,' Georgie snapped, and suddenly Alistair smiled as well.

'You know, you're sounding like me at the airport,' he said. 'Get on my bike or suffer the consequences. I didn't get on your bike and I suffered the consequences, so now I'm expecting you to be wiser. Right.' He stepped forward and lifted her into his arms in one swift movement. 'Lead the way, Gina. I'm taking this lady to X-Ray and then I'm taking her to bed.'

Maybe it had been the wrong thing to say. Georgie's face turned crimson suddenly.

'To your sickbed,' he amended. 'Don't look like that. OK, I know we were introduced in very different circumstances six months ago, but we're adults. Let's get a bit of professional detachment here. I'm sure we can handle it.'

* * *

He might be able to handle it. She couldn't. Safely tucked up in bed—Gina had ignored her protests, helped her off with her clothes and insisted she stay where she was—Georgie had the rest of the afternoon to think about the events of the day.

She wasn't all that upset about being in bed, she conceded. She'd been shaken more than she cared to admit. The punch to her face had done more than bruise her. It had brought back sweeping memories of the way she'd once lived—memories she'd spent her entire life fighting to get away from.

She was still feeling shaky. The X-rays were showing a hairline cheek fracture. She was getting slow in her old age, she thought bitterly, but it was still worth it. Smiley would definitely be going to jail. Gina had given her analgesics—'Humour me in this, OK, Georg?'—and she was grateful for them. They made her sleepy. She closed her eyes and let herself sink into her cool pillows, but sleep didn't come.

What came was the image of Alistair. A big man with gentle hands. The image of the way he'd held Thomas sprang to mind. He'd held the baby just as a baby needed to be held. Most men would be afraid of such a newborn, but not Alistair.

'He's still a prig,' she told her pillow. 'And he's still engaged.'

But she could see why Gina had asked him to give her away. He was a real father figure.

Um…actually not. There was nothing fatherly about the way she was feeling about him. He wasn't as old as she remembered. Mid-thirties? Young to be an eminent neurosurgeon.

The guy had to be seriously good.

But all the same…

'Stay away from him,' she told herself. 'He's only here for a week. I don't know why he upsets your equilibrium, but he does. Just keep clear.'

She finally did sleep, and when she woke it was dark. She was hungry, she decided. That had to be a good sign.

Her jaw ached. That wasn't such a good sign. She tried opening and closing her mouth a few times. She'd live, but she was in for an uncomfortable few hours.

The house was deathly quiet, apart from the whistling of the wind round the corners of the building. She lay still and tried to remember what day it was. Friday. The day before Em and Mike's wedding. There were celebrations taking place that night. Hens' night and bucks' night. Or a mixture of both, because there'd been hassles with the bridesmaids. Everyone who wasn't working would be down at the Athina.

They hadn't woken her. They'd have figured she wouldn't want to go.

She rose, flicked on her light and caught her reflection in the mirror. Wow. The bruising looked even worse than it had before she'd slept.

She needed Alistair and his camera.

Despite the discomfort, she grinned. This should really go down well in court. Hopefully by the time Smiley was released Lizzie would have her life together and would have found the strength to tell Smiley where to go.

A bruise in a good cause.

She got up and went to the bathroom, swallowed a couple of painkillers and returned to bed.

She was hungry.

As the painkillers dulled the ache, she grew hungrier.

They'd all be down at the tavern.

She didn't want to be at the tavern. She could do without noise and crowds tonight. But…

She had the fridge to herself, she thought, cheering up. Mrs Grubb, the hospital cook, kept their fridge laden and, as far as she knew, she was all by herself. Anyone who wasn't working would be at the party.

She pushed on a pair of scuffs as a concession to her sore foot—which wasn't all that sore—Alistair had done a decent job. Then she padded through the house, her stomach leading the way.

The place was in darkness. She flicked on the kitchen light and loaded a plate. Cold chicken. Quiche. Some sort of noodly salad. Apple slice—hoorah for Mrs Grubb. A glass of milk and she was set.

It was hot inside. Outside there was wind—an abundance of wind by the sound of it—but the veranda was usually sheltered. Clutching her plate, she pushed the screen door wide.

'Hi,' Alistair said, and she almost dropped her plate.

She wasn't dressed for company. She was wearing a very skimpy nightgown. Pink scuffs. Nothing else.

She retreated a bit but he'd pushed himself out of the ancient settee and was taking her plate from her.

He'd taken off his stupid suit. He was wearing shorts, a khaki, open-necked shirt and nothing on his legs and feet. He looked...amazing.

'I'll pull up a table.'

'There's no need.'

'There is a need,' he said gently. 'Hey, I'm not

going to jump you, Georgie. If you want, I'll even go away. You've earned the right to eat where you like tonight.'

'I didn't think you were going to jump me,' she said a trifle breathlessly, and he smiled.

'That's good, then. Sit.'

She sat.

'Are you hurting?'

'Gina gave me something. I'm fine.'

He nodded and went back to staring over the sea. Which gave her space to eat. It didn't hurt too much to eat. She still had space in her thoughts to watch him covertly. And think about him.

He wasn't a father type at all, she thought. Why Gina thought he could give her away....

She shouldn't be thinking like that. She tried really hard to concentrate on her food. Which was hard. It's the painkillers, she thought. They were making her fuzzy.

'Georg?' There was a yell from inside the house.

'We're out here,' Alistair called back.

It was Harry. He was still in his police uniform. Still on duty.

'I rang the bell and no one answered,' he said apologetically. 'Sorry, Georg. Your bedroom door was open so I knew you were up somewhere.'

'People come and go as they please in this

house,' Georgie told Alistair, as he looked confused. 'And Harry's one of us.'

'One of you?'

'The host of young professionals who run the Croc Creek rescue base,' she said. 'Medics. Policemen. Pilots. We're a huge team. Why aren't you at the party?'

'Duty,' Harry said bitterly. 'Plus this storm. I've been on the radio for the past hour, trying to persuade stupid bloody fishermen that they need to get into port right now. This cyclone's supposed to be blowing out to sea, instead of which it's lurking off the coast like a great black time bomb.' He sighed. 'Anyway, how's the face?' He flicked the porch light on. Then he flicked it off again. 'Ugh.'

'Hey, I have to be a beautiful bridesmaid in eight days,' Georgie protested. 'Say something bracing like, "Naught but a scratch, lass."'

'Naught but a scratch, lass,' Harry said, but he didn't sound convincing. He glanced at Alistair in indecision. 'Um…Georg, I need to talk to you.'

'I'm here.'

'About your old man,' he said, and Georgie stilled.

'What's he done now?' she whispered.

Harry hesitated. He glanced at Alistair, and Alistair obviously got the message. 'I'll leave you two alone,' he said.

But Georgie shook her head. For some dumb reason she suddenly wanted him to stick around. Strength in numbers? Something like that.

'Just tell me, Harry,' she said wearily, and both men looked at her in concern. 'I don't care who else knows.'

'He's wanted for a bank job in Mt Isa.'

She flinched.

'You didn't know?' Harry asked, watching her closely.

'No,' she whispered.

'He hasn't been in contact with you?'

'No.'

'But Max…'

She felt sick. 'Oh, God, Harry, I haven't heard from Max for months. I've been going out of my mind with worry.'

'Who's Max?' Alistair asked, and she flashed him a butt-out glance.

'He's mine!'

'Max is seven,' Harry explained. 'He usually lives here with Georgie but Ron took him away six months ago.'

'Which is why I drank too much at Gina's engagement party.' Georgie stood up, then leaned forward and grabbed the veranda rail for support.

Alistair was by her side before she reached the rail, holding her steady.

'I'm fine,' she muttered. She bit her lip and looked up at Harry, meeting his gaze head on. 'What do you want me to do?'

'Nothing,' Harry told her. 'I was pretty sure you hadn't heard but the big boys are telling me to ask you. Maybe they'll tap your phone.'

'If anyone phones me, it'll be Max. Not Ron. And they're more than welcome to listen to any conversation I have with Max. Where the hell is he?'

Harry shook his head. 'That's what I'm asking you.'

'Ron knows I'll kill him if any harm comes to Max.'

It was a flat statement of intent. She meant it. She shivered and Alistair was suddenly holding her close, hugging her against him.

'She's had enough,' he said, and Harry nodded.

'Yeah. I know that. I didn't want to ask. But you'll let me know, Georg.'

'If I hear, I'll yell it to the rooftops.'

'Even if it means jail for Ron?'

'You think I want him outside? Messing with Max? I want sole custody but they won't give it to me.'

'So you want him in jail,' Harry said, with a

lopsided grin. 'You're putting them all away tonight. I'll do my best to get him where you want him to be. Can I put out a missing person bulletin for Max?'

'Ron won't have deserted him. He wouldn't dare.'

'It can't hurt to broadcast that he's missing. People are more likely to respond to a plea for a missing kid rather than information wanted about Ron.'

'OK,' she said wearily. 'If it'll help… Please, Harry.'

'Leave it with me,' he told her, and then, with a last curious look from one to the other, he left them, striding down through the garden to the beach path below.

There was a long silence. The wind was rising to storm level now, bending the palms between them and the beach, whistling around the old house, making their sheltered veranda seem even more isolated. Even more of a refuge.

He should go in and leave her to her thoughts, but Alistair didn't want to. She'd pulled away from him. Now she was leaning on the veranda rail, staring at nothing.

He shouldn't get involved.

He was involved, like it or not.

'Your…Max left six months ago?' he said softly, and she didn't respond.

'Georgie?'

'Yeah,' she said flatly, at last. 'The night of Gina and Cal's engagement party. Ron just arrived and demanded Max go with him. He had the right. He took Max, even though Max was desperate to stay. Max is almost the same age as Gina's CJ. They'd just started to be friends. It was…' She broke off. 'Sorry. It's boring. Ron has the right and I don't.'

'So your behaviour the night of the engagement party….'

She rounded on him then, angry. 'I was drunk. I was out of my mind with worry. You don't think I really fancied you, do you?'

'I…'

'I was dumb, right?' she snapped. 'Get over it.'

'But you'll get Max back,' he said, thinking maybe he ought to leave it, but, regardless, he was compelled to keep going.

'If Ron's caught.'

'How the hell did you get caught up with a man like Ron?'

Silence.

'Georgie—'

'Leave it.'

'No,' he said, stupidly maybe, but, hell, he couldn't leave it like this. 'Georgie, I'm no expert but it seems to me the courts usually give custody to the mother. That's the way it is in the States at least, and I can't see why it's different here. If they granted Ron custody…well, maybe you were wild in the past. But there's enough people here who'd vouch for you now. You've got a great job in a terrific little community. If Ron goes to jail you could apply again…'

There was a deathly silence. He'd messed it up, he thought. He shouldn't have said it.

'You think I might have been a bad mother in the past,' she whispered.

'Hell, I don't know…'

'Just because I wear leathers.'

'They're great leathers.'

'But they put me in the right socio-economic class to be a bad mum.'

'Georg…'

'I'd slap you,' she said wearily, 'but I'm all slapped out. You stand there with your righteous answer-to-all solution. Prove to the courts that I'm respectable and… Hell, you think I should wear a twinset?'

She was close to hysteria, he thought.

'I think it'd be a damned shame if you wore a twinset.'

She stared—and then she choked, half with laughter, half with tears. 'You don't know what you're talking about,' she whispered.

'I do know you look fantastic.'

'In leathers. Every man's fantasy.'

'Actually, I was thinking you look fantastic in nightie, scuffs and bandages.'

'Cut it out.'

'Right.'

'You propositioned me last time you were here,' she whispered. 'Behind... What's her name? Eloise or something's back. Slime-ball.'

'You're talking about my fiancée?'

'Yeah, isn't that presumptuous of me? Low-life talking of her betters.'

'Where the hell did you get that chip on your shoulder?'

'If you give crazy compliments when you're engaged to another woman...'

'I'm not engaged.'

She blinked. 'Not...'

'There were...repercussions after the last time we met,' he told her.

'She found out? Someone told her? We didn't get past the hall door,' she said. 'Was that enough to make her call it off?'

'I called it off,' he said gently. Maybe it wasn't the time or the place to be saying this, but it suddenly seemed important that Georgie know. 'Eloise and I are solid professional colleagues who enjoy working together. We work long hours and it seemed an extension of that that we ate together and spent spare time together and finally moved in together. We just sort of drifted toward marriage. Only then…I came out here.'

'And you fell head over heels for me?' she mocked in incredulous disbelief. He shook his head.

'I hardly fell in love with you.'

'Well, you wouldn't.'

'Let me finish,' he said. 'Georgie, I was attracted to you. It was a crazy aberration and we have Gina to thank that it went no further, especially now I know what state you were in. But it did make me see that what I had with Eloise wasn't enough.'

'So I caused you to break off your engagement,' she whispered. 'Well, well. But you didn't say…'

'It was hardly appropriate to get off a plane shouting that I'd broken off my engagement. I didn't want to burden you with it.'

She blinked at that. 'Excuse me?'

'Yeah, that's presumptuous, too,' he agreed. Hell, he wasn't getting it right here. 'Look, I just want to tell you that I wasn't as big a slime-ball as you thought. Or maybe I was, but it was a big deal and what happened made me think through where I was going.'

She stared at him for a long moment. She raked her curls with her fingers and shuddered. The shudder made him move instinctively toward her, but she held up a hand as if to ward him off.

'No.'

'I'm not—'

'I know you're not,' she whispered. 'And I'm not either. But I am really, really tired.'

'I'll help you to bed.

'No,' she said. 'Thank you. I'll go on my own.'

'Is there anything I can do?'

'I don't think so.'

'If you think of any place you want searched,' he offered, 'I have a week before Gina's wedding. I was going to do some sightseeing but if you'd like me to help search for your son…'

'My son.'

'Max.'

She bit her lip. Then she whispered. 'No. Thank you. I don't know where to start looking and if Ron doesn't want to be found then he won't be. Even if I found them…I couldn't turn Ron in. I just…couldn't.'

'You still have feelings…'

'I don't have any feelings at all,' she whispered. 'Not for Ron. You're thinking he's my ex-husband. Well, that fits. Leathers, stilettos, bike, an ex-husband who's a criminal. Sorry to disappoint you but no.'

'Then…'

'Ron's my stepfather,' she whispered. 'He's the man who taught me to ride a punch. He's the reason I left home at fourteen and have never been back. And he's Max's father. My lovely Max. My kid brother. He calls me Mum because I'm the only mother figure he's known. He's the only male I've ever loved and ever will. Now, if you'll excuse me, I'm going back to bed.'

Out to sea, Hurricane Willie paused. For no good reason. The massive front of bad weather had been inching eastward. It had been expected to blow out to sea but now it seemed indecisive. It stilled, building strength. Building fury.

Even now the force from its epicentre was being felt by the mainland, from Brisbane to Cooktown. The mainlanders checked their weather charts and listened to the forecasts.

No one knew…

CHAPTER FOUR

GEORGIE wasn't at breakfast.

'I'm not sure where she is,' Gina told Alistair. 'She could even be sleeping in. This is an odd day. Georgie normally does an antenatal clinic out on Wallaby Island on Saturday morning but it'd be curtailed anyway because the wedding's at four. And now…this weather's so awful there's no way anyone's going out there.'

It certainly was awful. Alistair had been planning to take a diving trip to the Great Barrier Reef. Now he was trapped in Crocodile Creek, surrounded by wedding preparations for a couple he hardly knew.

'Maybe I should check on her,' he said, and Gina paused in what she was doing—was she really tying silver-painted chicken wishbones to baskets of sugared almonds?—and looked at him. Thoughtfully.

'Don't. She doesn't want you to. You upset her last night.'

'I didn't mean to,' he said, taken aback.

'She said you treated her like a tramp.'

'I didn't mean to do that either.'

'You suggested it was no wonder she didn't get custody of Max.'

'Hey.' He sighed and sat down at the kitchen table in front of Gina. And tried to think what to say. And couldn't. 'How many of these do you have to tie?' he said at last, which was pathetic but small talk had never been his forte.

'A hundred and twenty.'

'How many have you done?'

'Thirty.'

'And they're for?'

'Fertility. Mrs Poulos says.'

'Silly me for asking,' he said, and picked up a wishbone. 'Tell me about Georgiana.'

Gina kept on tying. 'She says you have her summed up.'

'I did have her summed up,' he said ruefully. 'I may have got it wrong.'

'She doesn't always wear stilettos,' Gina conceded.

'You mean she only did it for my benefit?'

'I suspect she was horrified about the way she behaved when you were here last.'

'I was pretty horrified at myself, too.'

'So have you apologised?'

'I… No.'

'She had a reason for behaving appallingly. What was yours?'

'I thought she was…'

There was a lengthy pause. Four more chicken wishbones got attached to baskets.

'You thought she was cheap?' Gina suggested.

'I thought she was gorgeous,' Alistair admitted. 'Cheap, yeah. But still gorgeous. When she threw herself at me, I couldn't resist.'

'Men!'

'She was…gorgeous. Trashy but great. You don't feel like that when you look at Cal?'

'Hey, we're talking about my future husband here,' Gina said with asperity. 'My husband in a week. Someone I respect. You're talking about someone you're describing as trashy.'

He winced. 'Are these wishbones for your wedding or for the one this afternoon?'

'This afternoon. Mike's mum read it in *Vogue* about a hundred years ago and she's had her heart set on them ever since. Every chicken that's gone through this kitchen has died for the greater good of Mike's wedding.' She tied another. 'So…' She looked at him dubiously across the table. 'You saw Georgie and you got the hots for her.'

'I'm sure there are better ways of framing it.'

'I don't have to watch my mouth with my cousin. Do you still have the hots?'

'No!'

'But six months ago…you felt so strongly that you went home and broke it off with Eloise'

'How do you know that?'

'Just because our mothers are dead, it doesn't mean I don't know your intimate secrets, Alistair Carmichael. Not that breaking off an engagement is an intimate secret. Why didn't you tell me?'

'It wasn't important.' He glowered. 'We're still friends and professional colleagues. So how exactly did you find out?'

'Georgie told me. She said you told her last night.'

She and Georgie had talked about him. That was…interesting.

'So why didn't you tell me?' Gina asked again.

'I didn't want you to—'

'To get the wrong impression,' she finished for him, suddenly thoughtful. 'You know, I'm starting to think there might be some other purpose in you agreeing to come here and give me away.'

'There's not,' he said shortly.

'No?'

'No.'

'But if Eloise is out of the picture…'

'Don't even go there.'

They went back to tying ribbons. Great intellectual exercise. It left Alistair's mind free to wander in places he didn't particularly want to wander. Finally they were interrupted. It was Gina's fiancé, Dr Cal Jamieson. He saw what they were doing and grinned. 'Hey, you've got another suck—I mean helper,' he told Gina. 'Well done, mate. Gina asked me to help but I was really busy. Lawns to watch grow. Imperative stuff like that.'

He got two wishbones thrown at him simultaneously. Followed by two baskets of almonds.

'Hey, don't both of you shoot,' he said, wounded.

'We're cousins,' Gina said briefly. 'It's called family support.'

'Why isn't CJ doing this?' Cal asked.

'He said it was boring.'

'Which it is—mate,' Alistair said, and rose. 'I've done twelve. That's my quota.'

'Actually, I have a job for you,' Cal said, turning serious. 'If you don't mind.'

'Anything that doesn't involve chicken wishbones and painted almonds. And I'm not even going to this wedding…'

'It's Georgie,' Cal said. 'She's over in the nursery. She and Charles are fretting about Megan. We want your advice.'

'I'm a neurosurgeon,' Alistair said, frowning. 'Advice?'

'She's hoping she doesn't need it,' Cal said, suddenly grim. 'But she's afraid that she might.'

Hell, this weather was wild. The moment they stepped out the door Alistair reeled back against the strength of the wind. Cal, who'd come out behind him, shoved his hands in the small of his back and pushed.

'Just a nice, gentle, ocean breeze, kiddo,' he said, grinning as both men put their heads down and battled the short distance to the hospital.

'My God... This is cyclone stuff.'

'Edge of a cyclone,' Cal agreed. 'Willie. But the weather guys are still saying it'll turn out to sea. They're predicting strong winds for this afternoon's wedding, but not as strong as this. It'll settle soon.'

'Do you often get cyclones?'

'Not bad ones. Or not often. Tracy took out Darwin on Christmas Day twenty years ago and one came through south of here last year and flattened the nation's banana crop.' He was yelling, but as he spoke they reached the hospital and walked inside. Cal's last couple of words echoed round the silence of the hospital.

'Why does Georgie want me?' Alistair asked. He knew this wasn't a social call. He knew she'd be avoiding him. So what now?

'She's worried,' Cal said. 'And Charles and I concur, but there's not a lot we can do about it. If this wind wasn't grounding all planes, we'd do an evacuation but…well, let's see what you think.' And he pushed open the doors to the nursery.

Charles was there, in his wheelchair. It hadn't taken long for Alistair to discover that Crocodile Creek's medical director was a really astute doctor. Charles had lost the use of his legs through an accident in his youth, but what he lacked in mobility he more than compensated for with the sheer breadth of his intellect.

Charles was a big man with a commanding presence, but right now Alistair hardly noticed Charles. For Georgie was beside him. The bruise across her cheek had darkened overnight and swelled still more. She'd removed the dressing he'd put over the split, and the cut looked…vicious.

They could throw away Smiley's key as far as he was concerned, Alistair thought darkly. Hitting a woman…

Hitting Georgia…

But they were standing by a cot, looking worried. He needed to focus on their problem.

'Cal said I might be able to help,' he said softly, and Georgie turned.

'Dr Carmichael,' she said.

They were obviously on professional ground here. OK, he could do that. He nodded. 'Dr Turner.' He nodded to Charles. 'Dr Wetherby.'

He looked down into the cot. Megan was lying on her side, one thumb pressed hard into her mouth. She wasn't asleep. But…

She was quiet. She was oddly still. First rule for care of children. Worry about the quiet ones.

And she looked so small. Malnourished? Probably. The cigarette burn on her hand looked stark and raw, and once again his gut clenched in anger.

No. Put emotion away. He was there for a reason.

'How's her mother?' he asked, still watching the little girl. They'd called him for something and he needed to figure out what. He was switching into professional mode, checking visually with care. Yesterday Megan had seemed lethargic. This morning he'd have expected her to be brighter. But she seemed apathetic. When he put his hand down in front of her eyes she blinked but didn't otherwise respond.

Hell.

'Lizzie's good,' Georgie said softly into the stillness. She was watching Megan's reactions as well. 'She's even managed a little breakfast. We've put Davy and Dottie into the ward beside her so they can see her as she sleeps, and she's a hundred per cent better than yesterday. Certainly she's out of danger. And so is Thomas.'

This was the benefit of a country hospital, Alistair thought. To combine medicine with family… It'd be great to be able to do these things.

'But you're worried about this little one,' he said.

'We are.'

'Tell me all you know.'

'It's not a lot but it's more than yesterday. Damn, we should have picked this up on admission.' Charles' words were almost a growl as he wheeled away from the cot to bring an X-ray back from the desk. He handed it to Alistair without a word.

Silence.

The X-ray showed the little girl's skull. With damage. The fracture was only hairline—no worse than the fracture of Georgie's cheek. But under Georgie's fracture lay muscle which could bear damage. Under Megan's skull fracture lay her fragile brain. Internal bleeding would be a catastrophe.

Internal bleeding may well be causing the symptoms they were worried about.

'Can I check?' he asked at last, and got three sharp nods for assent.

He crossed to the sinks and washed, carefully. Megan had survived the squalid circumstances of the hut. There was no way Alistair was risking infection now.

What infections did chicken bones carry? He washed twice as diligently as he normally did, and then he washed again.

Then he examined her. Cal left them, obviously needing to be elsewhere, but Georgie and Charles stayed. He ignored them. Instead, he talked to Megan, explaining gently that he was looking at her head, trying to find what was hurting her, trying to find a way to make her feel better. He wasn't sure that she was taking in anything.

He could see no retinal haemorrhage. That had to be a good sign. There was no obvious swelling.

'No fever?' he asked.

'No,' Georgie whispered. 'But…Charles didn't like the look of her. It was more on a hunch than anything that we did the X-ray.'

'Good hunch.'

'Which is when we bailed out and called you,' Charles said.

'Do we have the facility to do a CT scan?'

'Our radiotherapist is on his way in,' Charles told him. 'He's boarding up his mother's windows or he'd be here now.'

'Send someone else to board windows. I want him here now,' Alistair snapped. He closed his eyes, thinking things through. But his decision was inevitable. 'This little one was talking and re-sponding normally last night. The provisional di-agnosis is that she's bleeding internally, but slowly. If I'm right then we get in there now to try to stop lasting damage. There's no choice.'

We? Him.

He was under no illusion as to why Georgie had called him. He was a neurosurgeon.

But here…

He wanted a major city hospital. He wanted MRI scans. He wanted…

'We can't fly her out,' Charles said, sounding apologetic. 'Even by road we're starting to get worried. We've had a couple of big trees come down already, and the road's getting dangerous. They're saying it's worse down south—not better. With this level of wind it might be a few days before we can evacuate.'

'But we can't wait,' Georgie said. She looked terrified, he thought. She looked a far cry from the cocky, gum-chewing, bike-riding Georgie who'd greeted him at the airport yesterday. This morning she was wearing a professional white coat over jeans, T-shirt and sandals. Her sandals were crimson, matching her toenails. There were little gold crescent moons on each toenail. Despite her bruising, she'd gone to some trouble with her make-up—her lips matched her toenails.

There were traces of yesterday's Georgie left, but she looked young, vulnerable and afraid.

How could he ever have thought she was a tart?

'I don't want her brain damaged,' she said fiercely. 'I'll operate myself if I have to.'

She knew what the score was. Internal bleeding could cause—would cause—irreparable damage. The only option was to operate to relieve pressure, a tricky operation at the best of times, but here…

'You're not doing anything while we have Alistair. Gina says you're good,' Charles said grimly.

'Let's run a CAT scan first,' he said. 'I'm not doing anything on the basis of one X-ray. I don't have a clue where the bleeding is. We need to get a definitive diagnosis and I'm not moving without it. And then I need the equipment.'

'I suspect we have most of what you need,' Charles told him. 'Many of our indigenous people refuse to go elsewhere for treatment so if someone's available, we fly in specialists and they operate here. We've had a couple of neurosurgeons who've done locum work here, and they've set up a store of surgical equipment. If you weren't here, I'd have to ask Cal to do it. But he's a general surgeon. He doesn't have your level of expertise.'

'He'd still do it,' Georgie said bluntly. 'Will you?'

And the thing was decided. 'Of course,' he said. 'OK, get this radiologist here now. I'll check the scans, the equipment and the personnel available, and then we go. Let's move.'

If anything could take Georgie's mind off Max, this was it. Urgent, lifesaving surgery.

It had to be done. The CT—computerised tomography—scan showed very clearly a build-up of fluid, and when they shaved Megan's hair they could see swelling. Not huge swelling, but it was there.

Then there was a swift family conference. Lizzie was exhausted, but fully conscious and aware. She was appalled at what was happening to her daughter—but at first she couldn't believe Smiley would have done such a thing.

But the evidence was irrefutable. The white-faced woman held Davy's hand and trembled while Davy answered Georgie's questions.

'It was when Megan was hungry and Mummy was asleep,' Davy said, faltering. 'Megan started crying. Dad burned her with his cigarette and then when she wouldn't stop he hit her hard against the wall.'

For a moment Lizzie looked like she was about to pass out, but then anger took over and by the time Georgie explained exactly what the problem was, it was just as well Smiley was safely locked up.

'Just save her for me,' Lizzie said, close to tears. 'I swear he'll never lay a finger on her again but, please, Georgie, make her well.'

'We have Alistair,' Georgie said, and felt an almost overwhelming relief that this skilled surgeon was right here, right now.

She returned to Theatre to find everything was in place. Alistair examined Megan once more and then he nodded.

'We have no choice. We go in now or brain damage's inevitable. As it is…'

'I should have picked it up yesterday,' Georgie repeated, immeasurably distressed.

'There were no signs yesterday. All her symptoms could be explained by dehydration. They probably were caused by dehydration. I'm thinking this bleeding's gradual and slow, so we might be in time. There's no need to punish yourself over it.'

'So stop blaming yourself,' Charles told her. 'That's Georgie's specialty,' he told Alistair. 'She takes on the problems of the world and makes them her own.'

'Well, you're not on your own here,' Alistair said. 'Lizzie's OK'd the operation? If she approves, we go in.'

'We shouldn't ask you. You're not covered by insurance or medical indemnity,' Charles reminded him.

'But you are asking, right?'

'I guess we are,' Charles said, and managed a smile.

'But Lizzie wouldn't sue,' Georgie said, horrified.

'Smiley might,' Charles said.

'Alistair won't care,' Georgie said roundly, and Alistair met her look and held it.

'God knows, I have no taste for heroic surgery,' he said bluntly. 'I'd like a skilled paediatric surgical team on this one, but we make do with what we've got.'

'Maybe you'd better put your suit on first,' Georgie said faintly.

'Suit?'

'It makes you look clever,' she told him. 'Shorts and sandals don't cut it in the clever stakes and I want you to be clever.'

'So no stilettos, Dr Turner?'

She managed a shaky smile. 'No stilettos. Megan is too important.'

And after that there was no time to think of anything. There was certainly no time for Alistair to don his suit—he put on operating gear over his shorts and left it at that. Emily was called away from her hair appointment to perform the anaesthetic. Yes, this afternoon she planned to be a bride but 'I've got hours and hours and how long does it take to put on a dress?' Cal assisted Alistair and Georgie assisted Cal. Four doctors, three nurses and they were all needed.

That they all knew what to do was a testament to Alistair's skill. 'He does a lot of teaching,' Gina had told Georgie, and she believed her. For not only did Alistair's fingers move with skill and precision, knowing exactly what he was doing, improvising for any equipment he couldn't find with a dexterity that left her awed, he also seemed to know exactly what everyone else in Theatre was doing—where every person needed to be moments before they needed to be there.

His soft orders filled the room, and under his commands they worked as a team that a major teaching hospital could be proud of.

The procedure sounded straightforward enough, but what looked straightforward in textbooks was technical surgery of the most challenging kind. First he needed to lift a piece of Megan's small skull, working with infinite precision, aware that any false movement would aggravate the bleed. Then he worked carefully through the dura mater—the tough membrane around the brain—carefully separating the dura to locate the subdural clot causing the swelling.

After that he had to evacuate the haematoma and make sure there was no further bleeding from ruptured blood vessels. The skill lay in causing no more damage. This tiny brain was still developing. Any fractional miscalculation could have consequences for life.

Alistair worked as if this were a normal, everyday procedure. His demeanour was calm and methodical, as if this was nothing more serious than an inflamed appendix. But so much hung on his skill. OK, Cal would have tried to do this alone if Alistair hadn't been there, but as a general surgeon Georgie knew his chances at succeeding would have been much less. If all the bleeding vessels weren't located, the damage would continue.

Georgie knew instinctively that neither of these

things would happen after Alistair had operated. This man was just too competent.

Too competent for his own good? Ego driven? Maybe, she thought, but now wasn't the time to quibble about egos. He could be as egocentric as he liked, as long as he saved Megan.

And gradually it seemed that the combined skill of Alistair and Cal might do it. Hopefully they'd caught it in time. Hopefully there'd be no damage and Megan would grow up to be a normal, healthy kid like her brothers and sister.

Thanks mostly to Alistair. Georgie worked on with quiet competence, but inside she felt like weeping. They were so lucky this man was there. And to think she'd nearly abandoned him in the heat.

'Yeah, you still owe me for that,' Alistair said, as Cal carefully suctioned the wound, and she jerked her head up to meet his eyes.

The toad was smiling.

'You didn't want—'

'And you figured that was exactly what I'd do.'

'What are you guys talking about?' Emily queried, and to her fury Georgie felt herself blushing. She turned back to her tray of equipment, thinking, Dammit, did the man have a mind-reader on board?

He scared her witless.

But he was saving Megan.

Maybe he'd already saved her. The worst of the damage had been cleared. Now he waited patiently, taking his time, watching carefully for any ongoing haemorrhage. Then, satisfied that the area was dry, he began the laborious task of suturing the dura and reattaching the bone.

He left nothing to chance. His fingers were so skilful Georgie could only watch in awe. Hand him equipment as it was needed. Try to anticipate his needs. Marvel at the skill of the procedure she was watching.

Finally he moved on to the superficial sutures. Even that wasn't straightforward. For such surgery a specialist unit would have ready-made staples, but here Alistair could only suture, and the results of his suturing now would mean the difference between major scarring or whether Megan could wear her hair any way she liked as she grew up. Maybe such scarring didn't matter so much in the greater scheme of things—he was well within his rights to hand over to Cal for this last step—but Georgie could tell by Alistair's fierce concentration that he knew what scars could mean to a young woman. He was thinking forward to Megan's life after this surgery.

He cared.

There would be minimal scarring from this man's work today, she thought as he worked on. For a surgeon already weary from such an intense procedure, his sutures were flawless.

And then, finally, he could relax. They could all relax. Finally Georgie could hand over dressings, he could fit them over the child's neat wound and he and Cal could step back from the table.

'We'll need a further CT scan in a few days but it's looking good,' he breathed.

Only then did Georgie notice a trickle of sweat running down his face. The release of pressure… He'd held himself contained, until now.

There were advantages to being a control freak, she thought, but suddenly she was far from being in control herself. She was suddenly shaking. She stepped back from the table and leaned hard against the wall.

'Cal,' Alistair said urgently, and Cal was by her side, pressing her onto a nearby stool, pushing her head between her knees.

'I'm not fainting,' she protested weakly, for that was exactly what her body felt like doing. 'I never faint. Go back.'

'You've excuse enough to faint if you feel like it,' Alistair growled. 'Take her out, Cal. We're done here.'

'But we've succeeded,' Georgie whispered, and Alistair allowed himself the luxury of a smile.

'Yeah. We've succeeded. With a little luck—but not much, because this is as fine a job as any I've seen in major US teaching hospitals, and you picked it up so early that it's my guess she'll end up with nothing to show for this morning's dramas but a tiny scar.'

Georgie didn't answer. She couldn't. Why was she shaking now?

It was the bruised cheek and the drama of yesterday, she told herself, though she knew it was no such thing. It was a mixture of all sorts of stuff, not the least the way she was feeling about the man at the operating table.

He was way out of her league, but he was so…

'Go,' he said gruffly, and she looked up and her eyes met his. A silent message passed between them. Unmistakable. Go on. You've done well here. Look after yourself.

It wasn't said out loud but it may as well have been.

Why it made her eyes well with tears…

She didn't cry. She never cried. She wiped her eyes with an angry swipe and stood up. Once more she had to grab for the wall for support.

'Take her, Cal.'

Alistair sounded as if he wanted to take her himself, she thought, but maybe that was just wishful thinking on her part.

She glanced at him again. Once more that look…

She had to get out of there.

She went.

He found her twenty minutes later. Transferring a small child from the operating table to a bed in Intensive Care sounded on the surface an easy thing to do, but the attached tubing, monitors and assorted medical paraphernalia were complex. At this stage nothing was to be left to chance. Alistair had supervised it all. Finally free, with Cal doing the first shift of ICU watch, he went to do what every surgeon must. He went to tell the family.

Lizzie.

This woman had been living a nightmare. Hopefully now the nightmare would lift.

He pushed open the door to her ward and Georgie was there. Of course. And Davy. The six-year-old was sitting on the bed with his mother while Georgie was talking to them both.

'I thought I told you to go to bed,' he growled, and Georgie smiled at him.

'No. You just told me to go away.'

'I meant you to go to bed.'

'You're not my doctor—sir.' She was still smiling.

'My Megan is going to be all right?' Lizzie whispered. 'Georgie says she should…'

'She's not completely out of danger yet,' Alistair said, knowing there was no point in being less than honest. 'But the outlook is good.'

'Georgie's explained it to me,' Lizzie said. 'So I know.'

'It's great,' he said softly, smiling at Georgie, and she smiled back. The shaking had stopped. She'd regained a bit of colour. Basically back to normal?

Except for one smashed cheek and one missing kid brother.

'And I know what happened to Georgie's face,' Lizzie continued. Lizzie's strength was returning as the antibiotics took hold. Antibiotics had been flowing for twenty-four hours now, knocking the infection, and the difference was amazing. 'I hardly noticed her face this morning but now I have, and the police have been in to get my statement. But they said Smiley's going to jail, no matter what I say, so I may as well be truthful. It didn't make sense but then I saw Georgie's face. I really saw…'

'I ran into a door,' Georgie muttered, and put a hand to her cheek.

'Called Smiley. I know his punches. I can practically recognise his knuckle marks.'

'It doesn't—'

'He had it in for you,' Lizzie said, and the woman looked shyly up at Alistair, trying to explain. 'My last birth…with Megan, I bled and bled. I was OK in the end but this time Georgie told Smiley that if he didn't bring me into hospital when I went into labour she was going to use his testicles for fish bait. She said it real casual-like, and when he laughed she got quiet and said, "Don't push it, mate, 'cos I've got the entire Hell's Riders bikers' gang behind me and they don't like you any more than I do." So when I had pains he brought me in, just like it was his idea, but I know he hated it.'

'You need to leave him behind,' Georgie said softly, and Lizzie's eyes filled with tears.

'Yeah, but when he gets out of jail…'

'He won't be back for a while. With his suspended sentence, plus what he gets for this, it'll be at least a couple of years.'

'Even then…'

'Then you need to refocus,' Alistair said, watching Georgie thoughtfully. Maybe some things needed to be faced. 'You know that Georgie had it tough when she was a kid?'

'Hey,' Georgie said, astounded.

'You told me people used to punch you,' he said softly. 'So it seems you went out and got a black belt in karate.'

'I did,' she said, and she managed a smile.

'But Smiley still punched you,' Lizzie whispered.

'Only because you wanted him to punch you,' Alistair said.

There was absolute silence in the room at that. Davy was big-eyed, unsure of what was going on but smart enough to keep his mouth shut and listen.

And Lizzie figured it out, just like that. 'You did that for me?' Lizzie whispered.

'She did it to give you another chance,' Alistair said. 'Do you think you might take it?'

'Lizzie's tired,' Georgie interjected, embarrassed. 'We shouldn't be pushing it now.'

'There's never a better time to take a stand,' Alistair said. 'A line in the sand. Lizzie, yesterday Smiley was your dog-ugly, violent partner. Today he can be your ex-partner, a bad memory you can use the law to protect yourself from.'

'You reckon I could learn karate?' Lizzie asked, half-joking, but Alistair didn't smile and neither did Georgie.

'You can have your first lesson before you get

out of here,' Georgie promised. 'As soon as you're up to it.'

'I'd...I'd like that.'

'Then it's a deal,' Georgie said, and rose and nudged Alistair. Her message was clear. Lizzie had had enough.

'You've made my mummy better,' Davy said suddenly, snuggling down against his mother and smiling up at them.

'Would you like to learn karate, too?' Georgie asked, and the little boy's face lit up.

'I've seen karate on telly. Pyjamas and kicking. It looks cool.'

'It's also fun. You and your mum could have fun together.'

'Fun,' Lizzie whispered, as if it was a foreign word, and Georgie smiled and turned and left the room, leaving Alistair to follow.

He caught her before she reached the outer doors. She was sagging again, her shoulders slumping a little as she pushed against the glass doors. He caught her and pulled her inside again. What he wanted to say couldn't be said in the fierce wind.

'How much did you sleep last night?' he demanded, tugging her back and letting the doors swing closed again.

'Enough.'

'Not enough,' he growled. 'You're grey around the edges.'

'I am not.'

'Not outwardly but inside…'

'Oh, cut it out. You sound like Charles. Trying to make me stay in bed.'

'If Dr Wetherby was saying you need the day in bed, I concur.'

'I can't,' she said.

'Why not? Is anyone in labour?'

'No, but—'

'There you go, then. The entire medical staff of Croc Creek is stuck indoors, waiting for this weather to clear. Plus there are at least half a dozen spare doctors here for the wedding. Before Megan's drama Gina was so bored she resorted to putting ribbons around chicken bones.'

Georgie smiled at that. Albeit weakly. 'I should help her. And the wedding's at four.'

'No,' he said, gently but firmly. 'You need to sleep. No one's going to be upset if you miss the wedding.'

'I need to phone—'

'Who do you need to phone?'

'Anyone who might know where Max is.'

'Do you have a list?'

'I… Yes.' She gave a shamefaced smile. 'I sort of…found it last time Ron was here. When I knew he was taking Max away. He stayed overnight at the pub. I suggested to the publican that he might let me into his bedroom. I borrowed an address book he had.'

'You borrowed…'

'I copied out every phone number,' she said. 'Just 'cos I knew he was taking Max and I thought…'

'It was a great idea. You've been ringing the numbers?'

'Yes.'

'So how far through the list are you?'

'About a third.'

'No response?'

'No.' She bit her lip. 'Some of them recognise me. They know my stepfather hates me.'

'So I might get further?' he said thoughtfully.

'But you don't want—'

'I do want. I can contact people and say I'm a doctor who's deeply concerned about Max's welfare. I can say there are medical imperatives that make contacting him urgent.'

'Medical imperatives…'

'It'll make you sleep at night,' he said. 'Definitely medical imperatives.'

She choked, half with laughter, half with tears.

Then she took a deep breath, squared her shoulders and met his gaze head on. And came to a decision.

'It might work,' she said.

'I might get a better reception. A doctor saying there's an urgent medical need to contact a kid is bound to get a better reception than you looking for your father for a reason they don't know.'

'I... You're sure you don't mind?'

'I'll come and get the list. I'm not invited to this wedding. The weather's keeping me indoors. I have all the time in the world.'

They walked back slowly to the doctors' quarters. The wind was still howling. It seemed the most natural thing in the world for Alistair's arm to come around her waist and support her against its force.

They walked back inside the house—and stopped dead.

The house had been taken over by chaos.

There were bridesmaids everywhere—four or five at least—and a couple of flowergirls for good measure. There were three little boys in pale pink trousers and white shirts. There were women—lots of women. In the middle enveloped in white tulle was...

'Emily,' Georgie said, awed. 'Look at you.'

'I look like a toilet brush,' Emily wailed.

'Toilet brush?'

'Have you seen the toilet brushes Mrs Poulos uses? They're all white tulle. Just like me. Why did I agree to a Greek wedding?'

''Cos you fell in love with a Greek?' Georgie suggested, and grinned. Then her smile faded. 'Em, would you mind very much if I missed a bit of your wedding?'

'Not at all,' Emily said promptly. 'I'm with you. Shall we do a Thelma and Louise—fast car to Texas?'

'Not with Mike chasing us,' Georgie said. 'He'd catch us before the edge of town. You're committed now, girl. You need to face the music.'

'But your face is hurting,' Emily said, her expression softening as she took in the strain in her friend's eyes. 'And you're terrified about Max. Harry told us how worried you are.' She looked thoughtfully at Alistair. 'But you have Alistair to look after you.'

'I don't need looking after.'

'Hey, she does,' Emily said, pushing through assorted bridesmaids and flower girls to hug Georgie with affection. 'She's prickly as a hedgehog on the outside but inside she's just marshmallow,' she told Alistair. 'Georgie, go to bed. That's where you should be.'

'I need to make phone calls.'

'No, I'm making phone calls,' Alistair reminded her, 'while you rest.'

'That sounds like a great idea,' Emily said, but then she was distracted. A middle-aged lady in flowery Crimplene was hovering in the background with what looked like a crimping wand. The woman was practically vibrating with anxiety. 'No, Sophia, I don't want any more curls. I look like Shirley Temple as it is.'

'Hey, you need to get on with Operation Wedding,' Georgie said, and kissed her friend and pushed her away. 'I'll pop into church and see you tie the actual knot. But I might give the reception a miss.'

'If you decide you can make it, Alistair can bring you.' Emily looked ruefully around at the chaos. 'With this mob no one will notice an extra. Or a hundred extras.'

'I think we both might give it a miss,' Alistair said faintly, taking charge, putting his arm around Georgie and steering her through the sea of bridesmaids as he'd steered her into the blasting wind. 'Georgie's beat.'

'But we'll be there in spirit,' Georgie called over her shoulder. 'Make sure you save me an almond basket with wishbone.'

'They're for fertility,' Emily said, as the

crimping machine descended. 'You sure you want one?'

'We've changed our minds,' Alistair and Georgie said in unison. 'No fertility baskets.'

CHAPTER FIVE

ALISTAIR insisted that Georgie go to bed, but she refused. She wanted to listen to his phone calls. They compromised by using the hands-free phone, with him sitting in her bedside chair, gradually working his way through her list of names. The sounds of the impending wedding were all through the house—mass hysteria was a good description—and the rising wind made the sounds almost surreal. Inside Georgie's bedroom was an oasis of calm. Intimate even.

Which was the wrong way to look at it, Georgie decided as she lay back and watched Alistair work. She shouldn't be doing this, but there seemed little choice.

The painkillers Alistair had insisted she take were making her woozy. The panic of the last few hours was settling. Crazy or not, this man seemed a calming influence. 'Leave it to me, I'll take care of it,' he'd said. There was something to be said for big men. There was something to be said for men with gorgeous, prematurely silver hair and tanned skin and smiley eyes and...

And she'd had too many painkillers. Alistair was running through number after number and she needed to concentrate on what he was saying.

He made no mention of her. Alistair presented himself as Dr Alistair Carmichael, paediatric consultant at the Centre for Rural Medical Services in North Queensland. He obviously saw no need to mention that he wasn't actually employed here. He obviously saw no need to mention the name Crocodile Creek which, if her father had shot his mouth off about her, would be instantly recognisable to his mates.

What he said was truly impressive. Almost scary.

'We have urgent medical concerns regarding seven-year-old Max.'

That was about her, Georgie thought dreamily. Alistair's medical concern was that not knowing Max's whereabouts was interfering with her sleep and therefore medically undesirable.

'We understand Max's father is not in a position to contact us, but any help you could give us in locating his son would be very much appreciated. Any information will be treated in

utmost confidence—doctor-patient confiden-
tiality is sacrosanct. But it's imperative that this
child is located. Can I give you my private
number? If there's any information at all, we'd
very much appreciate it. If you can see your way
to help us or if you could pass a message to his
father to ring me…'

They'll think he's carrying cholera or something, she decided as he worked through the list.
It sounded scary.

As long as it worked.

It wasn't working immediately. Time after time
Alistair was met with negatives. 'But they're not
absolute negatives,' Alistair told her. 'Lots of the
numbers I'm ringing are private numbers and a
few wives and girlfriends of your stepfather's
mates have been answering. They sound concerned. They seem to know Max and I've got them
worried. Most of them have written my number
down and have promised to get back to me if they
hear anything. Hopefully I might have pushed
some of them to ask the right questions.'

It was the best he could do. Georgie lay back and
listened, letting the painkillers take effect, letting
her fear for Max recede. Everything that could be
done was being done. She didn't have to stir
herself. She was almost asleep…

'Megan,' she said once, rousing, and Alistair touched her hand in reassurance.

'She's fine. Gina just came to the door and told me. She's awake and seems more alert already, and that's with the effect of the anaesthetic not worn off. We think we've won. When this list is finished, I'll check again.'

Wonderful. Megan would be OK.

She was so close to sleep.

The last phone call was made. She should tell Alistair to go. She didn't need him there. But...

But she didn't tell him to go. The sensation of someone picking up her burden of responsibility was so novel that she couldn't argue.

He was there. He was...nice?

She slept.

He should go. He'd finished the list. He'd done what he'd set out to do. Hopefully he had people asking questions all over the country, trying to find the whereabouts of one small boy.

Georgie was asleep. There was no point in him sitting beside her bedside any longer.

But he sat on. Outside was the chaos of the impending wedding. The wind was gathering strength—hell, he was starting to disbelieve the reports that this cyclone was blowing out to sea.

How strong did wind have to get before it was categorised a cyclone?

He glanced out the window at the grey, storm-tossed sea and the palms bending wildly in the wind. This was amazing.

He glanced back to Georgie's bed, and he ceased thinking about the wind.

She was beautiful.

She was messing with his head.

She'd messed with his head six months ago, he thought grimly. He'd been happily settled, engaged to Eloise, paying a brief visit to Gina to make sure things were OK in his cousin's world. He'd met Cal and approved the match. He'd stayed on so he could make a family speech at their engagement party.

He'd met Georgie.

He'd actually met her earlier on the day of the party. She'd been sitting on the veranda of the doctors' house, drinking beer straight from the bottle. He'd talked to her for a moment. She'd sounded aggressive, angry, but also…frightened? It was a weird combination, he'd thought. He hadn't realised she was a doctor. He'd thought somehow then that she was a woman in some sort of trouble.

It had been a weird assumption, based on

nothing but the defiant glint in those gorgeous eyes. He'd tried to talk to her but she'd been curt and abrasive, shoving off from the veranda, making it very clear that he'd been intruding in her personal space.

Then that night…she'd turned up to the party in a tiny red cocktail dress that would have done a streetwalker proud. It had clung so tightly that she surely couldn't have had anything on under it. She'd worn those gorgeous red stilettos, fabulous hoop earrings and nothing else.

She was so far from what he thought was desirable in a woman that he shouldn't have even looked. He liked his women controlled. Elegant. Like…well, like Eloise.

But he couldn't keep his eyes off her.

Then as the night wore on she approached him. He'd suggested—tentatively if he recalled it right—that they dance. She'd tugged him onto the floor, put her arms around his neck, started moving that gorgeous body in time to the music, close against him…

Alistair's world was carefully controlled. He'd learned the hard way what happened when that control was lost. How many times had he heard his father use that dumb line—'I just couldn't help myself.'

Yeah, well, he could help himself, until he held Georgie in his arms, until he smelt the wild musk smell of her perfume, until he felt her hair brush his cheek…

He picked her up and carried her out of the hall. That, too, was partly at her instigation. 'Do you want to take me home, big boy?'

It had been a really dumb line. A total cliché. But it was an invitation he couldn't resist. She held him tight around the neck and she let her knees buckle so he had no choice but to sweep her up into her arms. And carry her outside…

It was just as well Gina saw them go. His cousin moved like lightning, furious with him, concerned for her friend, acting like he was some sort of ghastly sexual predator.

'She's in trouble,' Gina told him. 'She's not acting normally. She's vulnerable. Leave her alone.'

It was like a douche of iced water. Waking him up from a trance.

He left Georgie to her. He walked away, thinking he'd never see her again. But thinking… vulnerable? How the hell did Gina figure that out?

The next day, halfway through Gina's tour of the hospital, they walked into the midwifery ward and there she was. Georgie Turner. Obstetrician.

He'd assumed she held some sort of menial job at the hospital. But an obstetrician. He was stunned.

She didn't speak to him. He walked into the ward and she walked out. Once again he felt belittled. Guilty for a sin he hadn't had a chance to commit.

He should have got over it. And he was, he thought, gazing down at Georgie's face on the white pillow. He didn't want anything to do with someone as needy as Georgie.

But things had changed. When he'd returned to the States things had seemed different. His relationship with Eloise, seemingly so suitable, had suddenly seemed cloying. Dull?

A month later he'd told Eloise he couldn't go through with it. Not because of Georgie—or not directly because of Georgie. It was just that Georgie had showed him there was a life on the other side of control. He hadn't wanted it, but it hadn't been fair to Eloise to settle for her as an alternative. Eloise had hardly seemed disappointed, staying friends, accepting his decision with calmness. That had been great. That was why he admired her so much. He wanted that level of control.

He had it—except when he saw Georgie.

He couldn't stay to watch Georgie sleep. It didn't make sense.

But he wanted to stay.

'It's no use wanting what we can't have.' It was his mother's whiny voice, echoing from his childhood. When his father had disappeared in a cloud of gambling debts, taking off with a woman half his age, his mother's voice had moved to whine and had never returned to normal.

'You keep your life under control. You make sure—make sure, Alistair, any way you know how that you never put yourself in the position where you can be humiliated so much you want to take your own life. I'm so close to suicide… All I have is you. Oh, Alistair, be careful.'

It had been a dreadful threat to hang on a child, but Alistair had known she'd meant it. If he'd threatened her nice stable existence—her pride in her son…

Well, he hadn't. He wouldn't even now, when his mother was long dead. So what the hell was he doing, staring down at this sleeping woman and thinking…?

He shook himself. He wasn't thinking anything that'd worry anyone, including him. This was jet-lag. Exhaustion after this morning's operation. Concern for a woman who had more than she deserved on her shoulders.

So get a grip, he told himself, but he let himself

look at her for one long moment before he stood and walked slowly to the door.

And left her to her sleeping.

This wind was getting frightening. As Alistair walked out into the living room a shutter slammed off its hinges, hit the wall, broke off and tumbled crosswise past the house. He heard its progress, not falling but being blown. It was a big shutter.

One of the assembled bridesmaids screamed.

There were so many bridesmaids, still clustered. Apparently they'd dispersed to get their make-up done and now they'd regrouped. How long did bridal preparations last? The photographer was trying to get them lined up but was having trouble.

Gina waved to him from the back row. He hadn't recognised her until now. Pink tulle?

'It's ridiculous,' she said, abandoning the photo set-up and sidling out of her spot to join him. 'Poor Em.'

'Didn't she plan this?' he said, staring at…pink?

'Mrs Poulos planned this,' she said. 'Sophia. Mike's mum. This is a big Greek wedding, just as she's always dreamed of. Em loves her too much to say no.'

'I never thought I'd see you in pink tulle.'

'Apricot,' she retorted.

'Right. Apricot.'

'Sophia wanted the men in apricot dinner suits with apricot and white frills on their dinner shirts. But Mike put his foot down at that. They're in black tuxes.'

'Cal, too?'

'Cal, too.'

'And for your wedding?' he asked in a voice of deep foreboding, and she chuckled.

'If I asked you to wear apricot ruffles to my wedding, would you? Cousin?'

'No,' he said, revolted.

'Not even if I said please?'

'There's no love in the world great enough to encompass apricot frills.'

'Or red stilettos?' she teased him, and he stopped smiling.

'Gina…'

'I know.' Her smile widened. 'It's none of my business. But you and Georgie aren't slugging any more, I hope?'

'We were never slugging.'

'She's had such a hard time.'

'I'm starting to realise that.'

'Georgie's my only bridesmaid so you have to be nice to her.' She grinned. 'And, I promise, no tulle.'

He smiled back. He was trying to think of Georgie in tulle and failing dismally.

'She's OK?' Gina asked.

'She'd be better if she knew where Max was. I've been ringing through a list of her father's friends.'

'She let you do that?' Gina's eyes widened.

'I offered.'

'Yeah, but Georgie…' She hesitated.

'Gina, get back in line,' someone yelled, and Gina sighed and shrugged and smiled.

'Duty calls. Come and watch the wedding.'

'I'm not invited.'

'This is Croc Creek. Everyone's invited. Come at least to the church. It should be fun.'

And they all left, just like that. The photographer abandoned his work as hopeless and the car drivers ushered the girls out to the waiting cars. They were almost blown off their feet as they ran from house to cars.

Then they were gone, and the silence was unnerving.

What to do?

He'd already offered to help out at the hospital, thinking all the doctors would be at the wedding. But apparently two young doctors had arrived only three weeks ago—two eager and skilled interns on a working holiday from Germany. Herrick and Ilse were more than capable of taking charge and calling for help when needed.

Maybe he could go for a swim. But the wind made being outside unpleasant. The pool was protected, but even from here he could see the surface was littered with plant matter.

He should… He should…

Stay here. But… Georgie was sleeping off the bruise to her cheek, as well as making up, he suspected, for the sleep she hadn't had the night before. The thought of staying alone in the same house with the sleeping Georgie was somehow unnerving.

He'd head out onto the veranda to read. But just as he was making that decision, Mr and Mrs Grubb arrived. They swept into the kitchen to deliver a couple of casseroles—'for the doctors' supper if they get called away from the wedding, poor dears, and there's that nice young German couple as well need feeding up'. They were ceremoniously attired in their Sunday best. Dora's hat was…amazing.

'Why are you still here?' Dora demanded, and she seemed almost offended by the sight of him.

'Georgie's asleep.'

'All the more reason for you not to be here,' she snapped. 'Is that the only reason you don't want to come to the wedding?'

'I'm not invited.'

'That's a nonsense. Everyone's invited and it's not proper for you to stay here with Dr Georgie. You could be anyone.'

'As if I'm going to—'

'You're American, aren't you?' she demanded. 'I know your reputation. Overpaid, over-sexed and over here. Go put a suit and tie on and we'll wait for you.'

Some things weren't worth fighting. Deciding that defending his national dignity wasn't ever going to work, he decided on the second option. It seemed he was going to a wedding.

And so was Georgie.

It only took him a moment to change into his suit and when he returned to the kitchen Georgie was there. She was dressed, demurely for Georgie, in a tiny suit. In her beloved pillar-box red. And red stilettos. The skimpy skirt and jacket showed every curve of her gorgeous body. She'd applied make-up skilfully over her bruise, and it hardly showed under dark glasses. She was…gorgeous.

He stood in the doorway and stared.

She turned and saw him. And grinned.

'I overheard,' she said, and she chuckled. 'I decided I'd better come to the wedding. Maybe I needed Dora's chaperonage.'

'You need to be in bed.'

'I'm too scared to stay in bed. Over-sexed, eh?'

'You shouldn't be scared,' he said sourly. 'I'm going to a wedding.'

'Me, too,' she said cheerfully, and linked her arm through his. 'Overpaid too?'

'That's from the war,' Mr Grubb said, disconcerted. 'It's what we said about all the Yankee soldiers. They're not like that now,' he told his wife. 'At least this 'un isn't.'

'I can see that. How nice.' Mrs Grubb had changed tack, beaming at the unexpected expansion in her wedding party. 'You make a lovely couple. My mum's best friend, Ethel, ran away with an American sailor. He bought her silk stockings and they lived happily ever after.' She poked Mr Grubb in the ribs. 'Silk stockings. That's the way to a girl's heart.'

'We have other things than silk stockings,' Mr Grubb said with dignity.

'What things?' Dora demanded. Then she relented and giggled. 'Oh, well, I guess you are OK in the cot.' Then at the sight of Georgie and Alistair's stunned expressions she choked back her giggles and sighed. 'Oh, what it is to be young. Look at the pair of you. Ooh, I hear Cupid in the wings.'

'Dora,' Georgie said, quelling her with a look. 'I'm only going for the service.'

'Me, too,' Alistair said, and Dora beamed some more.

'Yes, dear. And then you can walk home together after. If this wind settles, like Sergeant Harry says it's going to settle—which it's not going to. It's going to be a biggie. I said to Grubb just before we got dressed, I said, it's going to be huge. I can feel it in my waters.'

'Um…what are your waters talking about?' Georgie said nervously, while Alistair said nothing at all. He was feeling like he was having an out-of-body experience and it was getting weirder by the minute.

'Cyclone, dear, that's what I'm feeling, no matter what Sergeant Harry's telling us. Veering offshore indeed.' Dora puffed herself up like an important peahen—or maybe peacock with that hat—gathered her shiny purse and took her husband's arm. 'But no matter. We've weathered cyclones before and we'll weather them again. Now, then, Grubb, let's all of us go to this wedding. Ooh, I do like a good wedding. Mind, one wedding breeds ten more, that's what I always say, and this one's no different.' She cast a not so covert look at Alistair and then at Georgie. 'I can feel that in my waters as well.'

'You have truly impressive waters, Mrs Grubb,' Alistair said, feeling it was time a man had to take control and move on. He took Georgie's arm just as possessively as Dora held Grubb, and he smiled down at her. 'Let's go see if they're right.'

Which meant that they were together. They were driven to the church together. In deference to Georgie's wounded face, Grubb insisted on dropping them off right at the church door before he went to find a parking place. Georgie and Alistair were practically blasted into the church together. Of one mind, they turned to the back pews, finding seats in the most obscure corner of the chapel.

'How come you're not a bridesmaid?' Alistair whispered as they settled in their back pew, and Georgie poked him in the ribs.

'Shh.'

The wedding hadn't started yet. Céline was singing 'My Heart Will Go On' at the top of her lungs, courtesy of Mrs Poulos, who was in control of the volume button. There was time for a brief conversation, even if Georgie didn't want it.

'But everyone else is,' he said. 'I thought you'd be a shoo-in.' Then he frowned. 'Isn't this the song from *Titanic*?'

She giggled. 'Nothing stops our Sophia. No little iceberg could get in the way of this wedding.'

'So why aren't you a bridesmaid?'

'Mike has three sisters and two cousins who, according to Mrs Poulos, would be offended enough to cause a rift in the family for generations to come if they're not bridesmaids. Em had already asked Susie so that made six, and enough was enough. However, one of Mike's sisters left coming here too late—the storm's stopped her—so Gina's taken her place. This is amounting almost to a plague of bridesmaids. I'm going to be Gina's bridesmaid and that's one bridesmaid experience too many in my book.'

'But you are Em's friend,' he said, watching the clutch of men around Mike at the altar. There were almost more wedding party participants than guests.

'I come from the other side of the tracks from Em,' she said, and he blinked.

'You mean there's a reason you weren't asked?'

'No, I…' She shook her head. 'I shouldn't have said that. Em doesn't care.'

'That you're from the wrong side of the tracks.'

'Yes.'

'You mean you're illegitimate?'

'I mean my family's dole bludgers and petty crims.'

'But you're not?'

'Maybe not,' she whispered dully. 'But you can't escape your family.'

He thought about his mother. And then he thought he'd rather not think about his mother. 'That's a hell of a chip on the shoulder you're carrying,' he ventured cautiously.

She glowered. 'Deal with it. I know when people are patronising me.'

'I'm not patronising you.'

'Right.'

'You know, I'm not exactly blue blooded either,' he said, eyeing her with caution. 'I'm not so far from the other side of your tracks that you'd notice.'

'Says the eminent neurosurgeon.'

'To the eminent obstetrician.'

She tried to glower. He smiled. She tried a bit harder to glower.

He glowered for her.

She giggled.

It was a really cute giggle.

The bride was about to make her entrance. Mrs Poulos did her worst with the control button. Whitney at her finest. 'I will always love yoo-oo-oo…'

The church was festooned with apricot and

white ribbons, flowers and bows as far as the eye could see. It was…

'Very tasteful,' Georgie said, still giggling, and they rose to their feet as the priest motioned them all to stand. 'Someone should tell Sophia this is a farewell song. Why are you from the wrong side of the tracks?'

'Um…my parents didn't have much money.'

'Is that all? That's not the wrong side of the tracks. That's shabby genteel.'

'My dad went to jail. Embezzlement. He stole to feed a gambling habit.'

That made her pause. Her smile died. 'Your real dad?' she asked cautiously, and he nodded.

'Golly. You almost qualify.'

'Thank you,' he said dryly. 'So where's your real dad?'

'He lit out when I was four.'

'Mine lit out when I was fifteen. With a waitress from a burger joint, and a year's profit from AccountProtect First Savings.'

'Wow,' she said, and almost as a reflex she touched her face.

'He never hit me,' Alistair said. 'Did yours?'

'I… My stepdad did, yes.'

'So does that put you further on the wrong side of the tracks than me?'

She stared up into his eyes. Her gaze held. Suddenly her lovely lips curved at the corners and she chuckled again.

It was a good sound. A really good sound, he thought. And he felt pleased with himself. For just a minute she was putting aside her terrors for Max and her pain from her injured face, and she was enjoying herself.

And who could not enjoy this over-the-top wedding? Mike was standing at the end of the aisle, looking stunned. Nervous as hell, despite the array of assorted males supporting him.

This was ridiculous, Alistair thought. What a production.

And then the great front doors swept open. 'I Will Always Love You' had segued into a full orchestral rendition of the Bridal March and the guests turned as one to see the bride make her entrance.

Emily. The bride.

This was crazy. She was a powder puff of brilliant white sweeping into the church, with Charles Wetherby in his wheelchair beside her. Charles looked proud fit to burst.

Emily was seeing no one. She looked straight ahead until she saw Mike and faltered in mid-step.

Alistair turned to look at the bridegroom. And he saw the look that flashed between the pair of them…

The whole ridiculous bridal production faded to nothing. This was what it was all about, he thought, stunned. One man and one woman, committing to each other, with all the love in their hearts.

It was no wonder Em hadn't put her foot down over the apricot tulle. The apricot tulle was nothing.

This man and this woman loved each other.

He had been right to break it off with Eloise, Alistair thought suddenly with a flash of absolute certainty. Eloise would never have looked at him like that. And the way he'd felt about Eloise…

No. This was loving. Out-of-control loving, letting go, a leap of faith—and who cared about apricot tulle? It didn't matter. All that mattered was that they belonged together.

He didn't belong here, he thought suddenly. He felt like an impostor, an outsider privy to emotions he hardly understood.

Embarrassed—or maybe not embarrassed but caught in some emotion he couldn't begin to fathom—he turned away. He didn't want to intercept that look again.

He turned to Georgie.

She'd caught the look as well. Her face had changed. Her hands had risen to her cheeks as though to drive away a surfeit of colour.

Her eyes were filled with tears.

'Georg,' he whispered, but she shook her head fiercely, denying him the chance to say a word.

He wasn't going to say a word. He couldn't think of a word to say.

But tears were slipping down her cheeks. He felt in his pocket, produced a handkerchief and handed it over. Then, as she wiped her face, he took her free hand in his and held it.

What sort of man still used handkerchiefs?

It was a bit of an errant thought but it helped.

Why was she crying at a wedding? This was dumb. It was the stupid analgesics, she thought. It had nothing to do with the way Mike was looking at Emily.

She didn't do weddings. She didn't even do relationships. The only relationships she'd ever experienced had led her to disaster.

It was her own fault. She didn't know who she was herself. She was dumb. She'd go out with a lovely gentle fellow doctor. He'd treat her as if she were Dresden china and she'd feel… empty.

Did she want to be slapped around, as her mother had been?

Of course she didn't. But there were times when she'd be drawn into a relationship with someone…well, someone her stepfather might have thought a mate. Someone who treated her as she'd learned to expect. She hated that, and it never lasted but, still, at least she knew where she stood.

So she'd never fall in love with a good man? That thought slammed home, alarming her. She'd been sitting a mite too close to Alistair and now she edged away. He turned and looked at her and he smiled.

He had a killer smile.

He was still holding her hand.

Alistair was one of the Dresden china ones, she told herself, feeling suddenly breathless. She knew from past experience that such men couldn't make her happy. She'd make them unhappy.

So stop smiling now!

Look at the bride and groom. That was why she was here. Not to think about Alistair-Good-Looking Carmichael.

And not to cry.

Pull your hand away, stupid, she told herself, but she didn't.

The bride and groom were making their vows, softly but with all the sincerity in the world. Mike was smiling at his bride, making Georgie feel…

Squirmy.

'Soppy,' she whispered, sounding as dumb as she'd felt for her tears, and Alistair grinned.

'Yeah, real Romeo-and-Juliet stuff. Bring on the violins.'

'They're happy though,' Georgie whispered, giving them their due.

'But we know this love bit's dangerous.'

She frowned, thrown off balance. 'Do we?'

'Of course. You need to decide with your head.' The priest was talking about the sanctity of marriage, but way back here they could whisper without fear of being overheard. The sound of the wind whistling around the old church was almost overwhelming, so bride and groom and priest needed the microphone to be heard.

'Decide what with your head?' Georgie asked.

'Your life partner, of course,' he told her, warming to his theme. 'You and I are doctors. Scientists, if you like. We know the heart's nothing but a bit of blood-filled muscle. If it fails you might even replace it with a transplant.' He motioned to the bride and groom. 'So where do you think these two would be if their hearts were transplanted? Unless there's a fair bit of cool, calculated thought in the equation, then the marriage is doomed.'

'Hush.' But there was no need to hush. No one could hear.

But she needed to hush him. What was he saying—that she should choose one of the gentle ones? The guys her head told her were suitable, but her heart abandoned as they pushed the wrong buttons.

'So what do you—?'

'Hush,' she said again, becoming so flustered she wasn't sure what she was thinking. Concentrate on the wedding, she told herself. This was an overblown Greek wedding. The church was full of apricot and white tizz. The bride and groom were surrounded by a sea of apricot and white attendants.

It was over-the-top ridiculous.

It was lovely.

He was still holding her hand.

The head and not the heart?

Yeah, well, that was where she'd been in trouble in the past. The Croc Creek doctors' house was always full to bursting with medics from around the world. Doctors used this place as a base where they could put their skills to use in a way that was invaluable to the remote peoples of Northern Australia. Doctors came here to help. Or sometimes they came just to escape.

Like *her*?

Yeah, but she wasn't thinking about herself, she

decided hastily. She was talking about potential lovers. So there were plenty available.

No one else seemed to feel a lack, she thought dourly, looking ahead at Mike and Emily. Maybe it was only *her* who'd never seemed to fit.

They were kneeling for the blessing. There was no need to say hush. Georgie blinked back more stupid tears.

It was only because she was weak, she told herself fiercely. It was because she was worried about Max. It was because her face hurt.

Alistair's hold on her hand strengthened. She gave a feeble tug but he didn't release it.

She didn't pull again. She sniffed and kept listening.

Then there was a break as someone played a Greek love song, with the volume on full to drown out the sound of the rising wind. Georgie didn't understand all that much Greek but the way all the old ladies in the church sighed and smiled, she guessed it had to be something soppy.

And then came the moment they'd all been waiting for.

'I now pronounce you man and wife.'

They rose as the priest gave his final blessing. The groom lifted Emily's veil and kissed her, oh, so tenderly.

It was just lovely. She was feeling…weird.

'Very romantic,' Alistair whispered dryly.

'Be quiet,' Georgie said for a final time, and to her fury she felt tears start to well again.

'I'm sorry,' Alistair said, and he sounded startled.

'There's no need to be sorry,' Georgie whispered.

'No,' he said, and squeezed the hand he shouldn't be holding. The hand she shouldn't be letting him hold. 'There's not.' He looked down at her in concern as she swiped angrily at her eyes with his handkerchief. 'We'll find him, Georg.'

But she hadn't been thinking about Max. Her eyes flew upward to Alistair's. And something… connected?

Their gazes held. He was comforting her, she told herself furiously, but she didn't quite believe it. For this wasn't a look of comfort and the confusion she felt was mirrored in his eyes.

She tugged her hand away with a faint gasp and turned her attention resolutely back to the bride and groom. They were being hugged by their respective families in the front pews.

A slate came loose from the roof above their heads. It crashed down—the sound tracking its progress on the steep gabled roof above their heads. She winced. Alistair tried to take her hand again but she wasn't having any of it.

She gripped her hands very firmly together and kept her attention solely on the bridal party. The Trumpet Voluntary rang out—played by Charles. His splinter skill. The trumpet's call was pure and true, almost primaeval against the backdrop of the storm, and once more Georgie found herself blinking back tears as the bridal party swept by them on their way out of the church.

But then, as the doors swung open and the wind blasted in, the bridal party stopped in its tracks.

Another slate crashed down.

The surge to leave the church abruptly ended.

'We might rethink the exit,' the priest announced in a voice he had to raise. Having left the technology of microphones to lead the couple out of church, he now had to raise his voice above the sound of the wind.

'This has to be a cyclone,' Alistair said, and Georgie blinked and bought herself back to earth. Earth calling Georgie…What the hell was she about, crying at weddings? She was losing her mind.

She didn't cry. She never cried. Crying was for wimps.

Alistair's dumb handkerchief was a soggy mess.

'We're still copping the edges,' she managed,

hauling herself together with a massive effort. 'Despite what Dora's waters are saying, it's still only category three. Strong but not disastrous.' She winced as a particularly violent gust blasted past the church, loosening another couple of slates. 'Harry says the biggest problem is flooding inland. It's the end of the rainy season and the country's waterlogged as it is. We'll have land-slips.'

'As long as that's all we have.'

'Scared?'

'Yeah,' he said, and he grinned. 'This wind is really terrifying for a man with a toupee.'

She choked. It was lucky the combination of wind and trumpet was overpowering because her splutter of laughter would ordinarily have been heard throughout the church.

He grinned.

Her laughter faded. He looked…a man in charge of his world. He was wearing his lovely Italian-made suit. His silver-streaked hair was thick and glossy and wavy, just the way she liked it. His tanned face was almost Grecian, strongly boned, intelligent…

A toupee…

She couldn't resist. She put her free hand into his hair and tugged.

'Yikes.' This time they were overheard. The people in the last pew—great-aunts en masse by the look of them—turned in astonishment. One started to glare but Georgie was giggling as Alistair clutched his head, and the old lady's glare turned to an indulgent smile.

'It's lovely to see the children enjoying themselves,' she said in the piercing tones of the very old and the very deaf. 'Look at the pair of them, canoodling in the back pew like a pair of teenagers. These will be next by the look of them. Sophie said this doctors' house makes them breed like rabbits.'

Georgie's mouth dropped open. 'Canoodling,' she muttered, revolted.

But Alistair was chuckling. 'Come on, rabbit,' he said, and nudged her to the end of he pew. 'Let's get out the side door before everyone figures that's the only exit out of the wind.'

'If we duck out the side door, the great-aunts will think…'

'Yeah, but we don't care what they think, do we, Georg?' Alistair said. 'We'll just get another tattoo and say damn their eyes.'

'How do you know I have a…?' She paused. She swallowed. Alistair's grin became almost evil.

'Aha! So where?'

'It's none of your business.'

'I told you about my toupee.'

'It's not a—'

'I just have very good glue.'

'I'll pull harder.'

'If you show me your tattoo, I'll let you pull all you like. I'll even let you canoodle.'

They were at the side door. He was ushering her through it, his arm around her waist as he propelled her forward. Behind them the entire wedding party was crowding round while they figured out the protocol of getting the bride and groom out of the church where the main door was suddenly unusable and slates might crash down on their heads. They'd have to use the side door. But not yet.

'Em and Mike…you'll have to go back to the altar and start the wedding procession again.' It was Mike's mother in full battle cry. 'Charles, start the trumpet again, from the beginning. Bridesmaids, back into line!'

'No mere cyclone's going to get in the way of Sophia's perfect wedding,' Georgie said, giggling, and then they were out the door, propelled into the instant silence of the vestry.

Alistair closed the door behind them. The silence was suddenly…electric.

'Hey. Um…Maybe we should go back and get

in procession like everyone else,' Georgie said, suddenly breathless.

'But you're not like everyone else,' Alistair said, turning. He'd been holding her hand. By turning, she was against the wall and he was right in front of her, smiling down. 'You're different.'

'I'm not different.'

'Yes, you are,' Alistair said softly. 'You don't belong.'

She stared at him, confused. 'I do belong.'

'Why did you come to Croc Creek?' he asked suddenly.

'I got a job here.' He was so close…

'With your qualifications there's a job for you wherever you want to go in the world. Croc Creek's home for those who want to devote a couple of years to a good cause. Or those who want excitement.'

'That's me.'

'Or it's a refuge for those who are escaping,' Alistair said, as if he hadn't heard her. It was almost as if he was talking to himself. 'What are you escaping from?'

'I'm not.'

'I recognise the symptoms.'

'You're a neurologist, not a shrink.'

'I'm an escapee myself.'

'You…'

'I like a bit of control,' he admitted, sounding thoughtful. 'That's why I was engaged to Eloise. Only then I met you and I decided control wasn't everything.'

'Hey.' She was suddenly really, really breathless. 'How did we get to this? You're really saying I influenced you in breaking your engagement?'

'Of course you influenced me. Just the way I reacted… I'm not saying I want to take it further…'

'That's good because—'

'Shut up and let me speak,' he said, quite kindly. 'All I want you to know is that what happened six months ago was a really big thing for me. Huge. I don't usually proposition complete strangers.'

'You're saying that between us…'

'Something happened. Yes.' Something was certainly happening in the church behind them. They could hear Sophia giving directions right through the massive door. 'But I don't know what,' he said. 'And before you think this is a line, I need to say I'm not interested in doing anything with it. At least, I don't think I am. As I said, I like control and you don't make me feel I'm in control. But I also know… Georgie, I recognise you're running, so maybe you need to be honest enough to admit it to yourself.'

'Why?' She was suddenly angry. What the hell was he playing at, psychoanalysing her like this? For what purpose?

'So you can move on.'

'To what?'

'To…life? It's not all that scary.'

'Like you'd know.'

'I—'

'Look, I don't know what's happening here,' she muttered. 'You're talking about something I don't understand.'

'You do understand it,' he said, and before she could respond he tugged her into his arms. 'Or at least you understand that what's between us is…well, it just is.'

'It isn't,' she gasped.

'It's not?'

She should fight. Of course she should fight. This was crazy. What was she doing, standing in the vestry with the wedding party on the other side of the door, letting him tug her against him, letting him lift her chin, letting him…?

No. She wasn't fighting. For every fighting instinct had suddenly shut down.

Everything had shut down.

He was going to kiss her and she wasn't going to do a damned thing about it.

Alistair.

And that was her last sane thought for a long time. His lips met hers and everything faded to nothing.

Everything but him.

The feel of him… The strength of him… She was standing on tiptoe to accept his kiss—despite her stilettos, she was dwarfed—but he was holding her so strongly that it was no effort to stand on tiptoe. He was lifting her to meet him.

Alistair.

It was like some magnetic force was locking her body to his. This was how it had felt six months ago when she'd danced with him. He was a great dancer. So was she. The dance had been Latin swing, and they'd moved as if they'd been dancing together for years. But every time he'd tugged her against him, preparatory to swinging her away, twirling her, propelling her into the next dance move, she'd felt exactly as she was feeling now.

As if his body was somehow an extension of her own.

No wonder she'd wanted him to take her. No wonder…

But the time for remembrance was not now. Here there was only room for wonder. Room for him. He was kissing her urgently, as if he knew that this kiss must surely be interrupted. As indeed it must. But his fierceness seemed entirely appropriate. It was a demanding kiss, a searing convergence of two bodies, a declaration that this was something amazing, and how could she deny it?

She couldn't deny it. She allowed his mouth to lock onto hers. Allowed? No, she welcomed it, aching for his kiss to deepen. Her arms came around his solid, muscled body and held him to her. She kissed back with the fierceness that he was using as he kissed her.

Her whole body felt aflame. Every nerve was tingling, achingly aware of him. Every sense was screaming at her to get closer, get closer, here is your mate…

Her lips opened, welcoming him, savouring him, wanting him deeper. Deeper. The kiss went on and on, as if she was drowning in pure pleasure, and she was, she was.

Alistair.

He was all wrong for her. For so many reasons he was wrong. But for now he was right and she was taking every ounce of pleasure she could get.

Alistair.

But suddenly he was drawing back. He was holding her face in his hands, forcing them apart so he could look into her eyes. The confusion she saw in his matched her own.

'Georgie,' he whispered, and there was confusion there, too.

'Don't stop,' she begged.

'We can't—'

'Just kiss me,' she begged, and she linked her hands behind his head and tugged him down.

'Georg—'

'Just kiss.'

He smiled, that achingly wonderful smile that had her heart doing handsprings.

He kissed.

The sound of the trumpet crescendoed behind them.

The door of the vestry flew open.

And here was the wedding procession, diverted from the main door.

The priest came first. Then came bride and groom, as if propelled by the mass behind. Then bridesmaids and groomsmen and pageboys and flowergirls and guests after them, tumbling into their private space, funnelled into the vestry with the door to the outside still not open.

The priest stopped in shock. As did the bride and groom. There was a moment's blank astonishment.

Then…

'Hey, get in the queue, guys,' Mike growled as he held his bride close. 'Today is our day. Gina and Cal are next Saturday. You two can take the Saturday after.'

CHAPTER SIX

THE muddle forced them apart. Blushing furiously, Georgie disappeared into the crowd and Alistair let her go. She might be confused but he was even more so.

He fell back to the edge of the crowd and then made his escape.

He wouldn't go to the reception. He was too…disoriented? Plus he hadn't been invited. It was one thing to go to the wedding ceremony and sit unnoticed in the back of the church, he thought. Not that he'd been unnoticed, but this was the theoretical etiquette scenario he was talking himself through. It was quite another matter to go to the reception, where he'd be eating food prepared for other guests, mingling with people he didn't know…

Staying near Georgie.

And that was the deciding factor. As the wedding party had forced them apart, Georgie had paled. She'd looked up at him with such horror that he'd been unable to think what the hell to do.

Maybe he should have taken her aside, tried to discover what the horror was about and see if he could defuse it.

But she'd backed away as if terrified, and he'd thought…well, did he have any reason to inflict himself on her?

'Yes, because of the way I feel,' he told himself, battling the fierce wind as he made his way back to the hospital. The wind was blasting so hard against him that it hurt. There was rain just starting, and raindrops so hard that they felt like pellets. But in some strange way it made him feel better. He felt like fighting—but he didn't know what, and he didn't know why.

'If she makes me feel like that then maybe I need to get the hell out of here,' he muttered, but he knew he couldn't go back to the States. Not until after Gina's wedding. Next Saturday.

'As soon as this wind eases I'll go down to Cairns and just come back for the wedding.'

That made him feel how?

In control? Maybe, but control was ceasing to seem very important. What seemed important was the way Georgie made him feel. Like there'd been an aching void which he'd suddenly figured could be filled.

He was so confused. He'd go to the hospital.

Medicine was a way of burying himself, he thought. It left him in charge of his own world as he tried to fix the messes of everyone else's world.

He pushed open the nursery door and Charles was there. Charles Wetherby, still in his tuxedo.

'Why aren't you at the wedding?' he asked, and Charles looked up from Megan's cot and grinned.

'I've done my duty. I gave the bride away and I played the trumpet twice. I'll put my nose in at the reception later but one of the very few pluses of using a wheelchair is that if you say you need to excuse yourself for a bit, no one ever asks you why.'

'You were in the wedding procession.'

'Not me,' he said cheerfully. 'I hopped it—or wheeled it—out through the priest's changing room as soon as I finished playing. Not even Sophia saw me sneak away. Oh, Jill and Lily will come and find me soon and drag me back, but for now I'm sticking here. Using an invalid's prerogative. What's your excuse?'

'I wanted to check on Megan.' But Megan was sleeping soundly and there was no way he was waking her up.

'Megan is great. Ilse and Herrick have been keeping bedside vigil, but there's little need. Ilse brought Lizzie through in her wheelchair and she's had a cuddle. Thanks to you.' He put out his hand, took Alistair's and shook it firmly. 'We're more grateful than I can say. You know, we could really use a neurologist here. I know we could never match your US salary but...' He grinned. 'There may be other compensations. So any time you're free...'

'Thanks but, no, thanks.'

'I'm not asking for an answer yet. Give it more than a cursory thought before you refuse.' He eyed Alistair speculatively. 'So why aren't you at the reception?'

'I'm not invited.'

'You know that makes no difference. And Georgie...'

'Yeah,' Alistair said heavily. 'Georgie.'

'So you're figuring it out,' Charles said, straight-faced.

'Figuring what out?'

'That you two are dynamite together.'

'Hey, there's no way. We've only just met.'

'You met six months ago.'

'For one night.'

'And Georg went round with a face like thunder for days. She'd take that bike out on the back roads south of here and come back with her gas tank empty and her bike and herself covered in mud. We had no idea what was driving her...'

'Her brother had gone.'

'Yeah, but that had happened before. She'd never been like that.'

'Charles...'

'Yeah, I know, butt out.' His pager sounded and he glanced at it, sighed and smiled. 'Women. That's Lily. My foster-daughter. It seems she's stowed boxes of confetti in the pouch at the back of this chair and my presence is required immediately. Or my confetti.' He wheeled back from the cot, smiling. 'OK, I'll head off to the reception. You know, Georgie isn't much of a one for parties,' he said thoughtfully. 'I might send her back to join you.'

'Don't.'

'She got one hefty slug yesterday. As her treating physician, I've advised quiet time. Sitting in the nursery with you should be just the ticket.'

'I'd prefer—'

'To be alone. Yeah, wouldn't we all? But look at me. I walked alone and now I have a partner and a child and all the accoutrements of life. They just sneaked up on me while I wasn't looking, and aren't I glad they did.'

'I don't want—'

'You don't know what you don't want,' Charles said enigmatically, and wheeled to the door. 'Keep Megan safe. And do consider my offer.'

'Offer?'

'Of a job,' he said patiently.

'I don't want—'

'You don't know what you don't want,' Charles said again. 'Think about it some more.'

And he disappeared, leaving Alistair alone with his thoughts.

It was dim and quiet in the ward. Megan was the only child in the nursery. Ilse came in and talked to him for a bit, but her English was poor. She kept throwing longing glances at the desk and finally he checked what she'd been glancing at and grinned. The title might be in German but he could recognise a romantic novel when he saw it.

'Go back to your book,' Alistair said, handing it over with good humour.

'It's that it's so quiet,' she said apologetically, smiling back at him. 'Herrick is bored as I. Everyone is at the wedding or—how you say?—banging wood on windows. Is there to be a cyclone?'

'I don't know.'

'I think a cyclone will be exciting,' she said, with the placid pleasure of the young. 'But you…you need to be at wedding. I can take care of Megan.'

'I'll go in a minute.'

'We have money,' she said, and she smiled. 'Ten dollars my Herrick has put.'

'Ten dollars?'

'Dr Luke has started…what you call…a book,' she said. 'That you and Georgie by the end of the week… Two to one.'

'What—?'

'So you need to go back to wedding,' she said. 'Because ten dollars is ten dollars and I don't want my Herrick to lose.'

'Go back to your romance,' he growled.

'And you, too,' she said, and grinned. 'Doctor.' And she buried her nose in her book before he could think of a suitable retort.

Weddings sucked.

Oh, as weddings went, this was a good one. Mike and Emily were a match made in heaven— even cynical Georgie had to admit that. The Pouloses' over-the-top enthusiasm was infectious, their generosity amazing, and it would be a strange person who couldn't be drawn into the fun and excitement. Even the wind, blasting around the little hotel in ever-increasing strength, seemed to be there specifically to form a backdrop to the band.

Georgie danced until her legs ached. She threw the odd plate with gusto. She ate a little.

She didn't want to be there. She wanted to be…with Alistair?

Don't do it, she told herself fiercely. You don't do love. You don't do commitment. You don't know if he's a gentle one or a bully, but they always turn out one way or the other in the end, and you know you can't bear either.

It could be fun to find out.

No.

Her current dance partner, Bruce, the local wildlife officer, spun her in a clumsy attempt at waltzing. She thought back to Alistair's expert dance techniques and that had her even more confused.

So why don't you want to find out? she asked herself.

'Because he's perfect right now.'

'Pardon?' Bruce broke into her conversation and with a start she realised she'd been speaking aloud. 'Who's perfect?'

'Um…' Not him, that's for sure, but how to say it and not hurt him? Bruce was a nice guy. One of the gentle ones. Except in the dancing department. Her toes had been squashed more times than she cared to think about. 'The little girl we operated on this morning,' she said, and he nodded.

They were approaching the corner of the room. Time for a tricky manoeuvre. Bruce put his tongue out just a little, his forehead puckered in concentration, and he swept her round.

There went another toe.

'I keep thinking of my work, too,' Bruce told her. 'Did you know Big Bertha laid her eggs right near the town bridge? Now I'm gonna have to fence off that part of the river till they hatch. Nothing like the vengeance of a mother croc if anything threatens their kids.' He paused, deciding to wait while another couple spun past them. 'Speaking of which...where's your little tacker? Where's Max?'

'With his dad.'

'Yeah, but Harry said—'

'Harry shouldn't have said anything,' she said curtly.

'Well, he didn't, so to speak, but of course he told Grace and Grace told Mrs Poulos and Sophia told me. You know things can't be kept quiet in this town. Hell, Georg, if you want a hand to hunt the bugger down...'

He would help, too, Georgie thought, forgiving him her squashed toes. This whole town would. They were all there for her.

The music ended. Bruce looked eagerly toward the bar. 'You want a drink, Georg?'

'No. Um, my face is hurting a bit. I might go home,' she said.

'There's still the speeches.'

'No, I think I'll go.'

'Alistair's back there, is he?'

She took a deep breath. They knew. Of course, the town knew. Any hint of gossip was around the town practically before it happened.

'I'm going home to bed,' she said with an attempt at dignity.

'Yeah?' He grinned. 'But I was asking—'

'I know what you were asking. Don't.'

'Course I won't. OK, I'll be off and find myself a beer. You don't want a ride home?'

'No.'

'Good, 'cos this is a great party. See ya,' he said with his accustomed good humour. 'But, you know, I've laid money the other way, so I'd prefer it if you could keep away from Carmichael. Ten quid's worth keeping.'

She turned around and Alistair was there.

'Hey,' Bruce said cheerfully. 'She was just going home to bed and you. Seems she doesn't have to.' He gave Georgie a friendly push toward Alistair, chuckled and left them to it.

The band started again. Fast swing.

'Hi,' Alistair said. 'Would you like to dance?'

'Dancing with you is dangerous.'

'I know,' he said, and he smiled. 'We both

know. But what's life if we can't live dangerously?' And suddenly she had no choice at all.
Alistair was tugging her into a rumba and she
simply let herself go.

There was nothing like dancing with an expert.
There was nothing like dancing with Alistair.

Dancing was wonderful.

Georgie's mother had loved dancing. From her
tired, life-battered mother, dancing was the last
thing anyone might expect, but May had loved it.
She'd given up on hoping for dancing skill—or
even interest—from the various no-hoper men
she'd ended up with, but as a toddler Georgie had
learned to be her mother's partner. When things
had got too ghastly she'd learned to turn on the
radio and plead with her mother to dance.

In the end illness and poverty had taken the
dancing out of her, but May had left her daughter
with a legacy she loved.

And Alistair's skill matched her own.

They danced like competition dancers. Every
move he made she knew and matched and melded
with. They didn't speak. She was laughing, abandoning herself to the joy of the dance, every fibre
of her being responding to his.

Others on the dance floor were falling back,

clapping in time, cheering. She was hardly aware of it. She loved it. She loved…

No. She didn't love…anything. Just the dance…

The music ended. She was exhausted, having danced to her limit, laughing up at him while the room erupted in cheers.

'Where did you learn to dance like that?' she demanded.

'My dad insisted on dance lessons when I was a kid,' he confessed, smiling, and he knew she loved it as much as he did. 'Pretty silly, eh?'

'Not silly at all,' she said. 'We ought to have introduced your dad to my mum.'

'And added a few more complications to our lives?'

Her smile faded, just a bit.

What was she doing there? Bruce was watching her from the bar. She'd told him she was going home.

She should go home.

'I thought you weren't coming,' she said.

'So did I,' he said. 'But Charles said the dancing was excellent.'

'Yeah?'

'And you were here,' he said simply, and as the music resumed—this time a slow waltz—he took her into his arms again. 'I'm not sure where this is going but I sat over there and figured that if I stayed there and you stayed here then I might miss my chance to find out.'

She gasped. She tried to break away. But he was holding her tight against him. Her treacherous body was moving in time with his, melding to his.

She succumbed to the dance.

She succumbed to Alistair.

And, as if on cue, the lights went out.

Just like that, the room was blanketed in darkness. The sound system died and the last twangs of music from the band sounded tinny and echoing.

'Is this a hint?' someone said from the floor. 'Is it time for the bride and groom to go to bed, then?'

There was laughter but it sounded a bit nervous. For all the assurances they'd had that the cyclone would miss them, the locals were starting to make up their own minds.

Alistair didn't release her. For some dumb reason she didn't want him to. She stood in the centre of the room while everyone else grew scared, and she felt…safe.

Within the secure hold of Alistair's arms she could look out and see what was going on.

'Harry…' It was Charles, calling from the doorway, and his tone was urgent.

There was still some dim light—each table had a candle. Some candles had gone out, but people were using the lit ones to relight others. Soon there was enough light to see by.

Cal came through from the veranda, seeking them out specifically.

'What's wrong?' Georgie asked, seeing by his face that there was real trouble.

'There's been a bus accident up in the hills behind the town,' he told them. 'Martha and Dan Mackers saw the Mt Isa bus go past half an hour ago. Just after it passed they felt what they thought was an earth tremor. Given this weather, it's a wonder they ventured out at all but they thought they'd take the Jeep down and check. They didn't get far. The road's collapsed just south of their place and the bus is on its side down the cliff. That place is a dead spot for mobile coverage so the report's been brief—Dan had to get back to his place to phone in. So we have no idea what we're facing. Charles is briefing Harry now. Can you two get back to the hospital?'

'I'll come with you up the mountain,' Georgie said, hauling herself out of Alistair's arms and stepping forward. 'Of course I'll come.'

'No,' Cal said. 'I was with Charles when the call came and we talked it through. Yes, we'll want medics on the mountain, but we want only the experienced emergency guys. We've had an upgrade on the cyclone. It's veered. We're right in its path and we're expecting to be hit by morning. The hospital has to be prepared for multiple casualties and the code black disaster response is activated right now.'

'Code black?' Alistair queried.

'The big one. Major external threat. I'd rather go,' Georgie said.

'Not going to happen,' Cal snapped. 'Not with that face. Charles wants you here, Georg—apart from him, you'll be the most senior doctor staying put if I have everyone else I want. Alistair, can we count on your help?'

'Of course,' Alistair said, as if it was a no-brainer.

'Then the reception's off for now,' Cal said ruefully. 'Every able-bodied man, woman and child in this town has a job to do right now. A cyclone with a crashed bus thrown in for good measure…'

'Oh…' It was a wail from Sophia Poulos, mother of the bridegroom. She'd been standing open-mouthed as Charles had explained to people at his end of the room what was happening. But Sophia's wail caught them all. 'Oh… This is bad.'

But the mother of the groom was nothing if not resolute. She took a deep breath, gazed fondly at the bride and groom and nodded. 'But of course you need my boy,' she said. 'And our Emily. Who else can look after these people? Emily, let me find you something else to wear.' Another deep breath. 'All this food,' she said, and she clucked. 'All this lamb. I'll tell the chef to start making sandwiches.'

At least she didn't have time to think of Max. Or Alistair. Though even that thought meant that she was thinking of them both. Back at the hospital they were in full crisis mode. The back-up generators meant they had power, and they needed it. Every available person was set to work, securing anything that could be an obstacle. Boarding up the windows was the first line of defence, but it was assumed that they might break open and nothing in the wards was to be loose to become a flying threat.

A receiving ward was set up fast. Any patients not on the critical list were sent home if their homes were deemed secure, or moved to a safe haven—the local civic hall—if they weren't. Of the remaining patients, those in the wards with the largest windows were shifted to the south side, out of the direct blast and hopefully more secure. The storerooms in the centre of the buildings that had no windows at all became the wards for the most seriously ill—the patients who, if the worst came to the worst, couldn't get out of bed and run for cover.

The theatres were windowless but Charles wasn't giving them over for ward use.

'Even if there are no injuries from this bus crash, if this turns into a full-blown cyclone we'll have trauma enough. I want additional linen, stores and pharmacy supplies in Emergency, Intensive Care and both theatres. Move.'

A big storeroom at the back of the doctors' house was used for back-up medical supplies. Charles wanted everything brought into the main building. Everything.

'I don't want to run out of bandages and not be able to get at more,' he growled. There were six elderly people in the nursing-home section of the hospital. Charles had them sorting and stacking as if they were forty instead of ninety, promising them they could rest at the civic hall when they'd finished.

Amazingly they rose to the occasion. Everyone did. Including Alistair. Georgie was supervising storage, making sure she knew where everything was so it could be easily reached. Alistair was one of those doing the ferrying of gear from the doctors' house. He was using a car to travel the short distance but even so he was soaked to the skin. Every time she saw him his clothes were soggier. His beautiful suit would be ruined.

They passed each other without speaking. There was no time for speaking. The threat was rising with every howl of the wind.

She couldn't locate the oxygen cylinders. Where were they? The normal storeroom was now a ward, housing Lizzie and her four children. Megan's cot had been wheeled in there as well, and Georgie paused in her search to check on her little patient.

She was still sleeping but she was looking great. A quick check on the notes at the end of the cot indicated she'd woken up and had a drink and smiled at her mother. Fantastic. Thanks to Alistair.

But there were problems. Lizzie was sitting bolt upright in bed, looking terrified. 'Georgie, is the jail secure?'

'You're worried about Smiley?'

'I don't want him to be killed,' Lizzie muttered, and Georgie abandoned her task and crossed to the bed to hug her. She included Davy and Dottie in her hug.

'Of course you don't,' she said, understanding. 'Smiley's the kids' dad. He's been your husband. Of course you're worried.'

'I don't hate him enough to want him killed.'

'We checked.' Help was suddenly there from an unexpected source. Alistair was standing in the doorway, dripping wetly onto the linoleum. 'Charles has had people contact everyone this side of the creek, letting them know what's happening, making sure they're safe. Harry told him the holding cell's a prefabricated makeshift building and he's worried about it. So he's let Smiley out for the duration. Harry has the feeling Smiley thinks he might skip town, but he's not too worried—there's no way out of here until this is over.'

'But—' Lizzie said, and Georgie answered her fears.

'Don't worry,' she told her. 'Look where we put you. Smiley would have to walk through two wards to reach you, and the whole town knows his story. He'll be too busy saving his own skin to worry you now.'

'Do you care about him?' Alistair asked, and Lizzie flashed him a look of astonishment.

'Of course I care. He's the kids' father.'

'And you don't want to waste your time worrying about him,' Georgie said, understanding the young woman's fear. 'Which you would if you knew he was in danger. So now you can put him aside.'

'So where's your Max?' Lizzie asked.

Georgie froze. She'd been watching Alistair in the doorway. Looking at the way his shirt clung wetly to his chest. Just looking. But her thoughts were dragged sideways to her little brother.

'One of the nurses said Max was in trouble,' Lizzie said shyly. 'It's only…Davy got into a fight at school last year and Max stood up for him. I hate to think of him out there in this.'

'He's not out there.'

'No, but the nurse said you didn't know where he was.'

'He's with his father.'

'And his father's on the run? Oh, Georg…'

'We do get ourselves into trouble,' Georgie said, and gave her another hug. 'Who needs men? What a shame Max and Davy and Thomas will grow into the species.'

'They'll be nice,' Lizzie said stoutly. 'My Davy and my Thomas will be nice, caring men. I won't let Smiley turn them into thugs. And I bet your Max will be great, too.'

'He will be,' Georgie said.

'Georg, where do you want the extra stretchers?' Alistair asked, and if his voice sounded strained she was going to ignore it.

Back to work.

'In the corridors. We'll stack them near the

entrance so they can be grabbed easily by whoever needs them.'

'You think it's going to be big?' Lizzie asked.

Georgie shrugged. 'I hope not. We should miss the brunt of it.'

'But you think—'

'I think we have to be prepared. Do you need help with the stretchers, Dr Carmichael?'

'No.' He looked at her for a long, hard moment. 'I'm fine by myself.'

He disappeared the way he'd come.

'He's sweet on you,' Lizzie said, and Georgie felt herself change colour.

'No.'

'He is.'

'It's no matter whether he is or not,' she snapped. 'Like you, I always fall for losers. So if he's falling for me, he's a loser by definition.'

And then the casualties from the bus came in.

This was no minor accident. The driver was dead. The first grim-faced paramedics told them that, and told them also to expect more deaths and more life-threatening injuries.

It seemed they had a major disaster on their hands before the cyclone even hit.

The first ambulance brought in a woman with

multiple fractures and major blood loss and an elderly man who was drifting in and out of consciousness and showed signs of deep shock. Query internal bleeding? X-rays, fast.

X-Ray was in huge demand. Mitchell Caine, their radiologist, was supposedly on holidays, but his locum had been delayed by bad weather. Mitch had been dragged in that morning to assess Megan's scans, and now he was back again.

'I shouldn't be doing this, ladies and gentlemen,' he said as he worked his way through the queue of patients needing urgent assessment. 'I'm so tired I'm not dependable. Just double-check any results I give you before you operate. If I say right leg, check I'm not talking about an arm.'

But his X-rays and reports were solid and dependable. Nothing like a code black to make a man forget about holidays.

Hell, this situation was impossible, Alistair thought. One overworked radiologist and no one else for three hundred miles?

'No one's going to sue here,' Georgie told him as they worked on. 'Everyone does what they have to do.'

Which was why twenty minutes later Alistair, a neurologist, was in Theatre, trying to set a fractured leg well enough to stabilise blood supply to the foot. With Georgie, an obstetrician, backing him up.

There was no time to question what they were doing. They just did it.

With the blood flow established—Alistair had worked swiftly and efficiently and their patient could now wait safely until a full orthopaedic team was available to fix the leg properly—they returned to the receiving ward to more patients.

The second ambulance was there now, and a third, and there was a battered four-wheel-drive pulling in behind it.

There were patients everywhere, some walking wounded, suffering only bruising and lacerations, but others serious.

For all the chaos, the place was working like a well-oiled machine. Maximum efficiency. Minimal panic. Charles had divided his workforce into teams, but the teams were fluid, doctors and nurses moving in and out of teams as an individual needed specific skills.

Every medic in Croc Creek was on duty by now, including a nurse heavily pregnant with twins.

'Don't mind my bump,' she said cheerfully as they worked around her. She was cleaning and stitching lacerations with skill. 'Yeah, I'm ready to drop but I've told them to be sensible and stay aboard until this is over. Just hand me the stuff that can be done sitting down.'

There was more than enough work to hand over. This was emergency medicine at its worst. Or at its best.

'You know, if this had happened in my big teaching hospital back in the US, I doubt if we'd do it any better,' Alistair muttered as they worked through more patients, and Georgie felt it was almost a pat on the back.

For all of them, she said hastily to herself, but it didn't stop a small glow…

She was carefully fitting a collar to a man who'd been playing it hardy. 'I'm fine, girl,' he'd said. He'd come in sitting in the front of one of the cars but now he was white-faced and silent. Georgie had noted him sitting quietly in a corner and had moved in. Pain in the neck and shoulders. Query fracture? Collar and X-rays now, whether he wanted them or not.

There was a flurry of activity at the door and Cal was striding through at the head of a stretcher. 'Alistair, can we swap duties?' he called across the room, and Georgie intercepted the silent message that crossed the room with his words.

Uh-oh. Alistair was a neurosurgeon. If Cal wanted him, it'd be bad.

It was.

'Head injury,' he said briefly. 'We had to intubate and stabilise her before bringing her in. Mitch has already run her through X-Ray. His notes and slides are here. Georgie…' She was near enough for him not to have to call her. 'Can you assist here?'

'Mr Crest needs X-rays.'

'I'll take that over,' Charles called. He'd just finished a dressing and he wheeled over to take Georgie's place. He glanced across at Cal's patient and saw what they all saw. A laceration to the side of her face. Deeply unconscious. 'Jill,' he said to their chief nurse, 'you work with this one, too. That's all I can spare. Do your best.'

'She'll need you all if she's to pull through,' Cal said gravely. 'The notes are there, guys.'

Jill was already wheeling the trolley swiftly into a side examination cubicle where they could assess the patient in relative privacy. Alistair was working as the trolley moved, while Georgie skimmed through Mitch's notes.

The woman—young, blonde, casually dressed but neat and smart by the look of it—was limp on the trolley, lying in the unnaturally formal pose that told its own story. Her breathing was the forced, rasping sound of intubation. Such breathing always sounded threatening, Georgie thought as she read. As it should. It meant the patient wasn't breathing on her own.

'Show me the films,' Alistair said.

Jill flicked on the light on the wall and held them up.

He winced.

'We're looking at interthalamic haemorrhage.'

'Yeah,' Georgie said grimly.

'Glasgow scale?'

'It was five half an hour ago,' Georgie said, referring again to the notes. 'But Cal has it now improving. It might have been initial shock that drove it so low.'

'Either way, I want an EVD in now,' Alistair said.

An EVD. A line to drain bleeding into the brain to prevent build-up of pressure. It was in many ways a repeat of the operation he'd done that morning on Megan.

But that morning they'd had six in theatre. Now...

'Let's find out if we have anyone else spare,' Alistair said grimly, reading her thoughts. 'But we move regardless. If pressure builds up any more, we're looking at major brain damage. We may be too late already.'

And in the end it was all down to Alistair, Jill and Georgie. In another life Jill had been a theatre sister in a teaching hospital that housed the major neurological centre for the state. She proved invaluable here. She had to be Jill of all trades. Surgical assistant. Charge theatre nurse. Junior. Everything else.

Because, to her horror, Georgie had to give the anaesthetic.

'You can do it with your eyes closed,' Alistair told her.

'Are you kidding? I can't—'

'We have three operations running consecutively,' Alistair said bluntly. 'You know that so let's stop the objections and just do it.'

So she did it, and she needn't have worried. She'd done the basics of anaesthetics in medical training and she'd performed almost as many gynaecological operations in Croc Creek than she'd had hot dinners. Up until now she'd had an anaesthetist every time she'd operated, but she'd watched what they'd done and enough had soaked in to make this almost instinctive.

But as well as that she had Alistair. She'd watched him work on Megan and his skill had stunned her. This was more of the same, and the woman under his hands had just as much chance of survival as if she'd been transported to a major neurological surgical team within minutes of the accident occurring.

The response team out in the field had intubated the woman and administered drugs to reduce the swelling of the brain as it haemorrhaged. They'd saved her life, and now Alistair was doing his damnedest to save her intellect.

He worked swiftly, referring to the CT scans again and again, making sure he was working on the source of the bleeding, his fingers moving with the instinctive speed of the highly skilled. The magnificently skilled. And every time Georgie faltered about anaesthetic dosage he snapped orders before her question was framed.

And finally it was done. The woman was as safe as they could make her. As Alistair applied the dressings and the pressure eased, Georgie checked the woman's pupils once again. There was a flicker of response.

'Hooray,' she said in a voice that was none too steady. 'This might just work.'

'We'll keep her asleep for a while,' Alistair said. 'We'll leave her in an induced coma. We'll check with one of the anaesthetists before we do that, though. All I know is that I don't want her feeling any pain. If she surfaces now, she'll emerge to confusion and I'm not risking any movement.'

'We still don't know who she is.'

'That can wait, too,' Alistair growled, and he stepped back from the operating table and let Jill run a swab over his forehead. He'd been sweating while he'd worked. He'd done the work of a team of doctors, Georgie thought.

He was…

One of the nice ones, she told herself, feeling more and more…strange? Weird. Here she was in one of the biggest medical crises of her career and she was thinking about Alistair? And she wasn't just thinking about him medically.

'Nice work, Turner,' Alistair said, and he gave her a grin across the table that might just as well have been a caress, the way it made her feel.

She didn't fall in love with nice, gentle medics, she told herself fiercely—desperately. They didn't keep her happy.

Even if they were Alistair.

By the time they emerged, the chaos had faded to a more manageable rush. The anaesthetist had finished working with another compound fracture and was free to take over the care of their unknown patient.

Georgie and Alistair were able to take a break.

Maybe even to go home. The emergency room was clear.

'Charles got everything sorted fast,' Jill told them as they emerged. 'This cyclone's moved now so we'll get hit directly. They're saying by morning at latest. We'll all be wanted again then so Charles is saying if you're free now, go to bed. He wants as many of his staff rested as possible.'

'That's fine by us,' Alistair said, and took Georgia's arm and led her out into the corridor. She should resist. She should...

But she was capable of doing no such thing. She let his hand stay exactly where it was.

Nice.

The entrance was crowded, but not with people. Here was the baggage from the bus—a muddled heap of sodden belongings. Alistair steered her past and she barely glanced down.

But she did just glance. And saw...

'Oh, God.' It felt like her heart had stopped beating.

'What is it?' Alistair asked, but she was already fumbling through the pile to reach what she'd seen.

She wasn't wrong. She lifted a bag gingerly from the pile, using one finger as if it might disintegrate before her eyes. It couldn't be.

'Max,' she whispered, and suddenly Alistair was

beside her, holding her under her arm, looking down at her face in alarm.

'You're white as a ghost. Hell, Georg, what's happening? Are you ill? We shouldn't have let you work.'

'This isn't about me,' she whispered, and she had to fight to get her voice to work. 'It's Max. This is his backpack.'

'Are you sure?' he asked incredulously.

She'd pulled away, squatting on the floor, unzipping the bag with fingers that trembled. She peered in, then upended it entirely. A pair of faded pyjamas. A ripped windcheater with the name of a sports team on the back. Bulldogs. A couple of pairs of a child's underclothes. One teddy bear. Ancient. Minus an eye and with stuffing coming out one knee.

'Spike,' Georgie said. She lifted the little bear into her arms. 'This is Spike,' she said, and her voice had steadied. It was strangely calm. She turned to Harry, who'd just approached. 'Max was on that bus,' she said. 'His dad must have put him on in Mt Isa. Dammit, he should have rung. Harry, have you found any kids?' Her face suddenly blenched even more than before and she staggered backward so she was sitting on the floor.

'He's not…he's not one of the bodies, is he? Oh, God, please…'

'He's not,' Harry said, kneeling on the floor and gripping her hands. 'Georgie, I've been up there. We found no kids.'

'His dad... Ron's on the run. They might both...'

'I know Ron, Georgie,' Harry said. 'He wasn't on the bus.'

'But he might be hiding. He might—'

'Georg, any person in that bus would be far too battered to be thinking about hiding. And the wind's terrific. Your dad might be afraid of jail but there's worse things than jail, and staying out in the rainforest tonight would be one of them.'

'But Max is definitely there,' Georgie faltered. She looked up at Alistair. 'He is,' she said dully. 'This is Spike. Max has just stopped carrying Spike around but Spike's never far from him.'

'But there's also the shoe,' Harry said slowly, and behind them the phone rang.

'The shoe?'

'There's a child's shoe. It worried the guys at the bus. Hold on and I'll fetch it. I think we might have left it at the front desk.' He turned and walked swiftly away from them.

He should go, Alistair thought. He might be needed.

He wasn't leaving Georgie.

Georgie was staring straight ahead. 'I know he's there. I need to go.'

'You can't,' he said, appalled.

She looked up at him mutely and clutched the bear.

'I…'

He stooped to hold her. 'No.'

The phone was getting to him. Hell, it was two in the morning. This was the emergency entrance. He crossed to the desk and lifted the receiver.

'Dr Carmichael?' a woman demanded.

'Yes.'

'Charles said you were in Emergency,' she said. 'This is Fiona. I'm manning the phones here. I have a woman on the line who needs to talk to you urgently.'

'To me?' he said blankly, and then he thought, Two in the morning, it'd be someone from home. Eloise? Some drama with the team at home?

He glanced down at Georgie. She was holding the teddy like it was a talisman, staring out into the night, as bleak as death. But her face was closed. She walked alone, this woman. When she was hurt she closed herself off.

'Put her through,' he told Fiona, not taking his eyes off Georgie.

'Is that Dr Carmichael?'

'Yes,' he said. The woman sounded as if she was whispering.

'You rang me earlier asking about Ron's son. Max.'

'Yes,' he said, becoming more alert. 'Yes, I did. Can you give me any information?'

'It's on the radio,' she said. 'I couldn't sleep and I was listening to the radio. They said the Mt Isa bus has crashed. They're talking multiple casualties. They say—'

'Are you worried that Max is on the bus?' he asked, cutting to the chase, and Georgie stared up at him, her attention caught.

'He is. My husband said Ron got rid of the kid. I was just…' She paused and took a deep breath. 'Well, I never thought…not for a minute, not really, but Max and his dad stayed here a while back and he's such a little boy. Him and that dog. And Ron didn't care. So when he said he'd got rid… Anyway, I told my husband that if he didn't tell me what Ron had done with him I'd go to the police, so help me. My husband knows me well enough now to know I don't stand up to him very often, but when I do I mean it.'

'When Ron said he'd got rid of him,' Alistair prodded, and Georgie was right beside him.

'I didn't think…well, he is his father after all,

so he wouldn't… But if he had then I would have killed them both. But he said that Ron put him on the bus to his sister. Georgie. Max talked about Georgie all the time. Ron hated the dog but Max said Georgie would like him.'

'So Max is on the bus from Mt Isa,' Alistair said.

'That's what I said.' The woman was crying. 'Ron's on the run and we took him in for a bit and I hated it but I put up with it because of the kiddie. And my hubby wouldn't let the kid stay here. So he said he'd got rid of him and I made him tell me—'

'He was on the bus last night?'

'I don't know.' The woman was weeping. 'I nearly told you this afternoon when you rang but I was so scared. But he left here on Thursday and we're… Well, I'm not saying where we are, no names, but it fits and if he's on the bus, someone should know.'

'Thank you so much,' Alistair said gently. 'You wouldn't like to tell me your name?'

'No,' the woman said. 'I wouldn't.'

And the phone went dead.

Alistair turned to look at Georgie. 'It is him,' he said, but she already knew.

'Here's the shoe,' Harry said, walking swiftly back into the room. 'But it has to be too small to belong to Max.' Georgie grabbed it before he was two steps into the room. Harry was right—the shoe was tiny. It looked hand-painted, with a red painted fish whose eye was camouflaging a small hole.

'It's not his,' she said.

'Then whose?' Harry demanded. 'The guys found it up the back of the bus. But we've searched at least a hundred yards in all directions and in that country no one's likely to have gone further, least of all a child.'

'But it's not Max's,' Georgie said stubbornly, and shook her head. 'No matter. The backpack's his. I'm going out there now.'

'Are you kidding?' Harry moved swiftly between Georgie and the door, blocking the way.

'Max is up there,' she said. 'Get out of the way, Harry.'

'Georg, there's a cyclone hitting within hours. There's no way we're letting you go out to the bus site, even if you could get through, which you can't. A huge tree crashed down just as we got the last of the passengers out. We were lucky to get out ourselves. If I thought it was possible I'd go myself—walk in if I had to, maybe take a team in—but I can't leave the town right now. No one can. We don't know when this storm's going to hit.'

'I'll take my dirt bike,' she snapped. She tried

to shove Harry aside but he wouldn't move. He held her as if she was a featherweight, and her karate knowledge did her no good at all against the big policeman's superior strength.

'No,' Harry told her. 'You said yourself it's not his shoe.'

'Then there's two kids,' she snapped, and shoved him again. 'Let me past.'

'We have no proof, and it's suicide, Georg.'

'We do have proof,' Alistair said gently from behind them. 'Harry, we've just had phone confirmation that Max was definitely on the bus. Suicide or not, there's a child's life at stake. I'll go with her.'

The pushing stopped. Georgie whirled to face him, her face a mixture of anguish and fear. 'You can't.'

'Don't you start saying *I* can't,' he said. 'Harry, the tree's blocking the road, right? Who else in town has a dirt bike?'

'I have one,' Harry told him, making a decision and moving swiftly into organisational mode. They now definitely had one child out there, and maybe another. That was worth taking risks for.

He'd go himself, Georgie realised, if the safety of the rest of Crocodile Creek wasn't resting squarely on his organisational shoulders.

'It's in the shed, Georgie, fuelled up, key above the door…'

But Georgie wasn't listening. She was staring at Alistair. 'You really can ride?'

'I can ride.'

'You'd better not hold me back.'

'Stop arguing, you two, and get going. You don't have long,' Harry said. 'Watch your footing off road. These hills are old gold country and the place is littered with disused mine shafts. Don't take a step until you know it's safe. You've got a radio, Georg? Of course not. Take mine and I'll pick up a spare at the station. Your cellphone won't work out there.'

'We're going,' Georgie said. 'I have to get out of these clothes.'

'Stilettos might be a bad idea,' Harry said gravely, but he was saying it to their backs. They were gone.

Leaving Harry looking after them. With a tiny shoe still in his hand.

Could Alistair really ride? She hardly believed him but by the time she'd changed swiftly into leathers and sensible shirt and boots and fetched her own bike from the sheds at the back of the doctors' house, Alistair was in the sheltered fore-court of the hospital, complete with bike.

The bike was an oldie but a goodie. It'd handle rough stuff.

And maybe so could Alistair. To her further astonishment he was dressed as sensibly as she was—in leathers as well.

'Borrowed plumage,' he said as she wheeled up beside him. 'This stuff was by the bike and in this wind we'll need all the protection we can get. And I've organised gear.'

It seemed he had, and he'd rallied the troops. Jill came rushing out of the main entrance as he spoke. Crocodile Creek's charge nurse had a white coat covering her wedding finery, but she'd defiantly repinned an exquisite orchid corsage onto her lapel.

She was carrying two emergency services backpacks.

'Charles told me to equip these for you,' she said. 'Your bikes aren't geared for baggage. Energy drinks, emergency saline, painkillers, a small oxygen canister, collars—everything you might need but we hope you don't. Also there's a decent radio that will get through to here. Charles says it stays on your back whatever happens and keep us informed. Harry also said to tell you he had to abandon a vehicle on the far side of the road block. He left the keys in it so you might be able to use it or take cover there if the wind gets too strong. But Charles says get in there, take a look and get out again fast. And no heroics.' She paused for breath. And swallowed. Her fear was palpable.

'You're all right here?' Alistair said, feeling torn. He'd done all he could to alleviate cerebral pressure on the woman with the head injury but he was aware that there was maybe a score of other patients. But Max…And maybe another child. What could be more urgent than that?

'We're under control,' Jill said, recovering, and he could tell by her voice that she'd guessed his thoughts. 'Charles concurs. This takes priority or he'd never let you go. We've got so many doctors from this wedding that we're OK. Your job is to look after Georgie. And yours,' she said, turning to Georgie and giving her a swift but fierce hug, 'is to find Max. Charles says he'll move heaven and earth to get you custody from now on. Our Lily loves him. CJ loves him. We all love him. Bring him home safe.'

CHAPTER SEVEN

THAT was it. The time for talking was over. It took all their concentration and more to keep the bikes on the road. The road up into the mountains was steep, and that helped a little. The road had been cut into the mountainside, forming a sheer cliff to their left. The cliff gave them a little shelter—not much, but without it riding would be impossible. Even under the lee of the cliff, debris was already piling up. Rain was slashing into their visors. It was like a scene from a nightmare—and the cyclone hadn't yet hit!

Alistair rode ahead, inching his way through the mess, and Georgie was content to let him. It had only taken minutes for her to realise that he could do more than just ride a bike. The man was an expert.

So why had he refused her offer of a ride on the back of a Harley when she'd collected him from the airport?

Pride, she thought, trying to keep her mind on

anything but the thought of Max somewhere out in this storm. In his gorgeous suit Alistair would have looked pretty silly.

OK, one to Alistair. She was ready to forgive him anything right now. She'd have come alone, but now all she had to do was keep her bike on track behind his, keep him within sight, letting him do the initial assessment of the road and the obstacles in their way. To come here alone would be terrifying. But to have him in front...

Careful, she told herself. She didn't do dependence. Alistair was one of the gentle ones, intelligent, caring, nice...

Oh, cut it out. The man was a loner. As if he'd be interested...

And if he was, then she wasn't. Happy families? She didn't think so.

Where was Max?

Twenty minutes from home they found the tree. A massive gum blocked the road entirely. They pulled to a halt, propped their bikes and checked it out.

They didn't speak. The wind was terrific, hurling leaf litter everywhere, and the rain was almost blinding them. The sound of the wind was almost deafening in itself and taking off their helmets to make it easier to listen would be crazy.

Alistair grabbed her hand and towed her. She let him. The wind was so strong she felt she might be blown off the mountain if she didn't hold onto something.

And holding onto Alistair was...well, OK.

There was a way around. At the base of the tree, where the massive roots had ripped their way out of the rain-sodden ground, the land must have initially been almost clear. There was a passage of sorts around the roots. They could take their bikes through.

They walked it first, emerging on the other side to see, as promised, one of the hospital's four-wheel-drive trucks. If Harry had been driving it, he was lucky he hadn't been ten feet further along when the tree had crashed, Georgie thought. Hell...

'Will we go the rest of the way in the car?' she yelled to Alistair, and he shook his head.

'If one tree was down a few hours ago, there's bound to be more down by now. The bikes are our only chance. But stay close to me. Don't drop back more than ten feet.' He'd been yelling, too, and a sudden drop in the swirling wind made his voice echo. He grinned and, seemingly on impulse, undid his helmet clips, pushed up her helmet, did the same to his, tugged her close and kissed her gently on the lips. Then replaced his helmet as if nothing had happened at all.

'We'll find him,' he said softly. 'Come on, Georg. Let's go.'

The bus scene was chaos.

They'd been given careful directions but it wasn't hard to find. Ten minutes of careful riding past the fallen tree and there it was.

Or there it wasn't. The entire roadway had slipped, the slide having started from the cliff above, leaving the road a mass of sodden rocks and soil.

There were chains anchored to trees, disappearing down the slide. There were the marks of people—lots of people. The start of the slip was scarred with a mass of footprints, heavy boots, the signs of rescue workers involved in a massive retrieval operation.

They still kept their helmets on—it'd be crazy to take them off. Propping their bikes on the sheltered side of the road, they inched their way to the edge of the landslip, shining the powerful flashlights they'd been provided with.

Twenty feet below was the bus.

'It's stable,' Alistair yelled across the wind. 'The guys said it's securely fastened. They used cables to make it safe.'

'I'm going down.' And she was sliding down in the mud, not caring what Alistair was doing, forgetting Alistair completely. She felt sick. Somewhere here was Max. Somewhere...

If he'd felt like hiding when the rescuers had come then maybe he'd be back in the bus by now. That'd be the sensible place for him to be. Please...

She tried to hurry but Alistair was behind her, gripping her shoulder, hauling her back.

'You fall and break your ankle and there's all of us in a mess,' he yelled. 'And remember what Harry said about old mine shafts. We do this carefully and sensibly, Georg, or not at all.'

She tried to brush him off but his hand still held her.

'What's it to be, Georg?' he yelled. 'If you start being crazy, I'll pick you up and tie you to a tree till I'm done, and I'll search the place alone.'

'You wouldn't...' She whirled to face him, trying to shove his hand away.

'Try me,' he said.

She stared up into his face—and she knew she'd met her match. His face was implacable. Either she started being sensible or he'd pick her up and put her where she'd be safe. What he'd do to keep her there she didn't know, but this man wasn't to be crossed.

'OK,' she said, trying not to sound as shaken as she felt. 'But I stay in front.'

'No,' he said, and grabbed her hand. 'We do this side by side, Georgie, or not at all.'

So side by side it was.

Even when they got to the bus he stuck by her. The teams before them had smashed out the front and back windows, or maybe they'd been smashed in the slide. The bus was sprawled on its side, its floor facing the road. They reached the front window and Georgie put her hand on the frame preparatory to climbing in.

'No,' Alistair said, and hauled her back. 'Not until I check the cables. The guys said they were OK but I'm not taking anyone's word on it. I want to know this baby's secure.'

'You check the cables and I'll go in,' she screamed into the wind, desperate to find out, even if it meant finding out the worst.

For answer he simply tugged her sideways and took her with him.

The cables were OK. The bus seemed solid, but by the time Alistair finally acquiesced to climbing aboard she was almost ready to scream.

Inside, the bus was appalling. People had bled here. People had died here. There'd been no thoughts of clearing the mess—the rescue teams had moved as fast as possible to get everyone out and get off the mountain. Therefore the detritus of the rescue effort was still here. Dressing covers. Blood-stained clothing. A damaged saline bag, still half-full. And the rain was blasting in, soaking everything.

It looked like the scene of a massacre. They clambered inside and stood up as best they could and gazed around them.

Nothing.

No Max.

'Do you suppose he's under the bus?' Georgie asked, her voice faltering. Here inside the bus the noise of the wind was almost bearable.

'Harry says not,' Alistair said. There was no need now for him to be holding her hand but he was definitely holding it. It seemed a link that they both valued. 'The driver was caught underneath. They had to do a bit of levering to get him out—they did that last thing. But as they worked the bus moved again. It shifted over a tree stump before settling and they got a clear look underneath. They're almost a hundred per cent certain that it's clear.'

'But they're not absolutely a hundred per cent certain,' she said, swallowing.

'Let's not look for more trouble than we already

have,' he said, pulling her with him as he checked every seat in turn. Making absolutely sure a small body wasn't wedged somewhere it could have been missed.

No one. Nothing.

The radio crackled into life in Alistair's backpack. He let go of Georgie's hand to drag his pack off and retrieve it. He watched Georgie all the time, as if concerned she'd bolt. 'Yes?'

'It's Charles.' Charles Wetherby was curt at the best of times and he was brief now. 'You two OK?'

'We're in the bus. There's no one here.'

'We've been thinking. If it's Max, there has to be a reason why he'd run, right?' Charles snapped. 'He's a sensible kid.'

'Yes,' Alistair said cautiously. The radio was powerful—he didn't have to hold it to his ear and they could both listen.

'We've been talking to patients from the bus. Most of them seem to have been asleep when it crashed and there were a few stops along the way, so trying to figure who was on the thing is impossible. And the driver's dead. But there's an old lady who says she was sure there was a boy sitting up the back on his own. And there was another child with one of the women, though she can't remember who. But she said the two kids were playing with a dog. Harry found a dog lead in the pile of belongings. He's checked all the baggage now and he's saying there's a smaller child's clothing. So we treat it as confirmed. We have two kids missing, and it's too late to send in more searchers. But it's the dog I want to talk about. I'm guessing here, but if the bus crashed and the dog took off in fright, maybe the kids went looking for it. It's a long shot but it's all we have. If we'd known this earlier, I would have sent in a team regardless. Two kids in the bush in a cyclone doesn't bear thinking of, but you're on your own.'

'The woman who phoned,' Alistair said, thinking it through. 'She mentioned a dog. It fits.'

'Max doesn't have a dog,' Georgie said.

'We assume he has one now,' Alistair said. 'It's odd to think he'd have run away for any other reason, and the only other option is that somehow he's buried somewhere underneath the bus. We'll go with the dog option. Thanks, Charles.'

'Keep me informed and move fast,' Charles said bluntly. 'They're saying three hours before the worst of this hits, but it may be less, and I want you out well before that. With or without kids. I know it's hard but look after your own skins first. Georgie, I know you can't make that call so, Alistair, I depend on you to make it for her.'

And the radio went dead.

'OK,' Alistair said. 'Where do we start?' But it was a rhetorical question. He was already moving back the way they'd come in—the smashed front window. The normal entrance to the bus was somewhere under their feet. Useless.

'Hurry,' he said, and she didn't need to be told.

Then they were outside the bus. Even in the time they'd been inside the wind had worsened. The cliff was protecting them from the worst of its force but the treetops were being blasted. Within two minutes of emerging, they heard the splintering of branches.

'This is crazy,' Alistair yelled. 'Surely they'd have returned to the bus. They must be lost.'

Georgie was shining her torch around the scene, taking her time now, knowing she had to be careful. It was so dark. To find anything before morning seemed impossible

They had to try. 'If I were a dog...' she muttered, thinking it through.

'What?'

'I was thinking... If they were up the back of the bus, chances are they'd get out through the smashed rear window. So let's check the rear.'

They did. Nothing there. But...

'The land up to the road is really steep here,'

Alistair said, shining his torch around. The bush seemed impenetrable. 'If I were a terrified dog, I'd head for the nearest exit.' His torch swung slowly, searching, and Georgie joined hers with his. Then...

'There,' he said.

It looked like a creek bed. Or some sort of basic waterway. There were rocks along its base and there was a trickle of water under the stones. But the stones were big and packed close together, making it almost a track.

'If I wanted to get away in a hurry, that's the way I'd go,' Alistair said, and grabbed her hand and tugged her.

She went willingly.

But not as swiftly. Alistair was surefooted and fast. She'd thought he was a swank city surgeon, with his gorgeous suits and carefully groomed hair. But now...in his borrowed leathers and heavy boots he was as fast and as fit as any of the emergency service personnel Georgie knew in Crocodile Creek. He'd ridden the bike like an expert.

'Where did you learn this?' she demanded as they climbed swiftly from rock to rock. Every few feet Alistair stopped, shone his torch in all directions and yelled. Georgie tried it once but her voice was about a hundred decibels lower than Alistair's roar.

'College choir,' he said, shining his torch into the bush again. 'First baritone.'

'I meant the hiking. And the riding.'

'Abseiling's a hobby,' he told her. 'And there's not a lot of places you can abseil for joy without a bike.'

'Abseil for joy?'

'Abseil where you don't have half the enthusiastic amateurs of the country waiting for you as you haul yourself over the top.'

'You abseil alone?'

'I'm not an idiot. I do it with friends.' Her foot slipped a bit and he caught her before she hit the water. 'Careful.'

She didn't have to be careful when this man was here, she thought. He just took control. He just…

'But you do karate,' Alistair said. He tugged her up and her body met his momentarily as he steadied her. 'We're birds of a feather, Georg.'

'I'm not,' she said instinctively, and she felt rather than saw him grin.

'Deny it all you like,' he said. 'But it's there for all that. Damn.'

He stopped. She was slightly behind him. He still held her hand, and he tugged her absently against him as he shone his torch ahead. 'OK. Path ends here. What now?'

Maybe they ought to go back. The wind was

screaming so hard that if they hadn't been in the comparative shelter of the forest floor they wouldn't have been able to hear themselves speak.

Up until then the creek bed had formed what seemed almost a natural footpath. But now the stones stopped abruptly and the ground rose again. Alistair's torch picked out the flow of water and followed it. There was a natural cleft in the rising ground, and stones and water disappeared, almost buried.

'The water goes underground,' Alistair said, and raised his torch to shine it round. 'They must have left the path here.'

It seemed Alistair wasn't thinking of giving up yet, and neither was she.

'Surely they wouldn't have come this far.'

'If the dog got frightened and they were following it…like us, they'd have thought if they'd come this far they couldn't go back without trying to find him.'

'But where…?' Her torch joined his.

'There,' Alistair said, aiming the torch behind them and up a bit. There was a small break in the timber. 'We go in until it's blocked again and then we stop. Agreed?'

'OK.'

'You're worried about going in?'

'I'm worried about stopping,' she said, and tugged him forward.

Twenty yards. Thirty. The way was possibly the path of animals coming to drink—small animals. The path was clear to almost waist height but no higher. Alistair was using his hands to bush-bash, shoving the undergrowth aside to let her through. Georgie was holding both torches.

There was a crack like a shot from a rifle and a branch broke off above their heads, crashing its way down through the rainforest canopy to land ten feet ahead of them.

A cry.

Not theirs.

Georgie stopped as if struck.

Alistair had heard it, too. They stood frozen, almost afraid to move.

Nothing. Nothing but wind screaming above their heads and the driving rain.

Maybe it was an animal.

'It was a child,' Georgie said. 'I swear.'

'Wait,' Alistair said. He took his torch back from her and gripped her hand.

She waited. She was learning to trust him.

She'd come a long way in two days.

The wind was shrieking, making it impossible for them to hear anything else. Nothing. Nothing. But then came what Alistair had been waiting for. A tiny gap in the wind blasts, as if the wind was catching its breath to blast again.

'Max,' he roared into the night. 'Georgie's here. Yell back.' It was a yell to wake the dead and Georgie jumped almost a foot.

'Sorry,' Alistair said as the wind took up its screaming again. 'I should have warned you.' He gripped her hand again, warning her to stay silent.

She needed no second bidding. They stood hand in hand, waiting for another break in the wind. Alistair's arm came round her waist and he tugged her against him. Holding her steady.

No. Just holding her.

Waiting. Waiting.

The wind caught its breath…

And there it was. A yell, high and shrill, screaming through the bush.

'Georgie, Georgie, Georgie.'

Max. Dear God, it was Max.

The wind took over again but they'd heard enough. Close. To the right and up a bit. Past a break in the path…

Alistair was inching forward and Georgie was pushing him.

'Don't,' he growled, and his body formed a barrier so she couldn't go past him. She couldn't go faster.

And then…

'Hell,' Alistair said, and stopped dead. Then he was on his knees, on his stomach, lying full length on the ground, inching forward.

Astonished, Georgie followed him with her torch. And saw…

It must have been almost invisible. It still was. There was a mass of branches and leaf litter over the path, but there was a slit in the midst of it.

A yawning hole. It would have been disguised by leaf litter until someone had…someone had…

'Hold onto my belt,' Alistair ordered. 'And find yourself some purchase. I need to find the edge.'

She needed no second bidding. She knelt, grabbed the solid trunk of a sapling with one hand, then reached over and grabbed his belt with the other.

He was feeling with one hand, shining his torch with the other.

'There,' he said, tugging away a heap of leaf litter as Georgie helped to pull him back.

He'd exposed the edge.

A mine shaft.

The path they'd followed must indeed have been a path, made maybe fifty years ago when men had mined these mountains.

'Max,' she said, and it was a whisper. And then again but this time it was no whisper. 'Max.'

'Georgie.' It was half cry, half sob, and it came from deep within the mine. And then came the fierce yap of a dog.

Max. And dog.

Another blast of wind, so fierce this time that it rocked them, even in this sheltered place. There was another crack of splintering timber.

'Max, Georgie's here and I'm Georgie's friend. I'm Alistair.' They didn't need to discuss who was going to do the talking—Georgie's voice was way too weak. Pathetic, she told herself. She ought to do voice training.

'Max,' she yelled, doing her best. 'Max, I'm here.'

'Georgie…' It was a sob of terror.

'Who's down there?' Alistair boomed.

'Me and Scruffy and another kid.' Somehow the shaft made Max's voice echo, enabling it to be heard.

'Are you hurt?' Georgie yelled, and Alistair repeated it.

'Scruffy's got a sore leg. He keeps yelping. And it's cold.'

'The other kid? What's his name?'

'I dunno. It's dark.'

'Is he OK?' Alistair yelled. 'Is he talking?'

'He doesn't talk.'

'Is he asleep?' Oh, God, what was he asking? But Georgie knew what Alistair was asking, and she thought she didn't want to hear the answer.

But it seemed she did. 'He's hugging Scruffy,' he called. 'We…we sort of held hands for a bit when I cried. He's OK.'

Georgie saw Alistair's swift intake of breath. *'When I cried…'*

'Did you fall?' she yelled. Dear God…

'Scruffy fell in. The kid fell in after him. I stayed on top for a while and then I got really scared and I got too close and I sort of slid down on top of them. I hurt my knee a bit but it's not bleeding. But we can't climb out.'

Slid. Not fell. Georgie's breath went out in a whoosh. If they'd clear fallen…

'Max, is there another hole near you?' Alistair called into the shaft. 'I know it's dark but can you feel? Could you fall any further?'

'The bottom's made of rock,' Max yelled back. 'It's really hard.'

'Is there any water in there?'

'It's dry.'

She closed her eyes. How lucky had they been? They'd fallen into a shaft that had bottomed on rock and then been dug no further.

But how deep were they? Not so deep that she

couldn't hear Max above the wind. Not so deep…
Ten, fifteen feet?

'So you're all safe?' Alistair asked.

'We're stuck,' Max said in childish indignation
that Alistair wasn't seeing the clear picture. 'And
we're hungry. And Scruffy's hurt his leg.'

There was another explosive crack of timber.
Too close for comfort.

'I need to get a bit further out so I can look
down,' Alistair said. 'Can you hold me?'

'Of course.' She could have held back a ten-ton
truck right now if it meant getting Max to safety.

'Let's just check my belt buckle's tight first,'
Alistair said, and wriggled back a bit to check.
'This is Harry's gear and Harry's a bit wider than
me. I don't fancy plummeting down, leaving you
holding onto Harry's leathers.'

He was smiling. In a situation like this…he
was smiling?

Maybe he had cause, Georgie thought, letting a
little of the tension ooze away. The kids were safe.
In this fearful wind the bottom of a mine shaft was
probably the safest place for them.

And it seemed Alistair agreed. He wriggled
forward while she held on for dear life. He shone
the torch down and then he wriggled back again.

He'd hauled off his backpack and he reached for hers as well.

'Provisions,' he said.

'Provisions?'

He was hauling out a couple of bottles of drink, high-energy orangeade. A fistful of chocolate bars.

'Jill's done us proud,' he said. He was tugging off his jacket. 'They can both huddle under this.'

She stared at him. 'Don't be stupid. We'll get them out…'

'Not for a while. You want to donate your jacket as well?'

'I… Of course.' She tugged off her jacket. Damn, she only had a skimpy top on underneath. Alistair had a long-sleeved shirt.

Maybe she needed to do a rethink on her clothing.

But Alistair had moved on, shoving the jackets and provisions out to the edge of the shaft. 'Right, Georg, hold me again.'

She did so. He shone his torch down, carefully assessing.

'I can see you guys,' he called. 'Max, hi. Scruffy, hi. And you…' He was obviously talking to the second child. 'What's your name?'

No answer.

'He wasn't talking on the bus either,' Max said. 'I don't think he can.'

'But you're OK?' Alistair asked, and then seemed to relax. 'Max, I want you guys to push yourselves as far as you can away from my torch beam. I'm tossing you a few things to eat and drink, and two jackets to put on.'

'We want to get out,' Max quavered.

'See, the problem is,' Alistair called apologetically, 'that a cyclone's about to hit. A really nasty storm. Any minute, in fact. That's why the bus crashed—the storm before the cyclone washed the edge of the road away. Georgie and I had to come in on bikes, which means we haven't got ropes. We'll have to get some. But you're safe where you are. What Georgie and I will do is leave you this food. We'll go and find somewhere to keep ourselves safe, but as soon as you hear the storm ease we'll be back with rope to get you out. We promise. It'll be a few hours—maybe until daylight—but you have to be brave. There's no choice.'

'Don't go,' Max called, and it was a sob.

Georgie was still gripping Alistair's belt as if her life depended on it, but she was appalled. 'We can't.'

'We don't have any choice,' Alistair called back to Max, ignoring her protest. 'Max, this storm is awful. You and your friend and your dog are in the safest place in the country right now. If we could, we'd join you, but you're pretty squashed as it is, and I'd need rope to lower us down. So we have to leave.'

'Georgie,' Max sobbed.

'I'll go down to them,' Georgie said, but Alistair had pulled back. As Georgie pushed forward, he caught her and held her, as one might hold a child.

'No,' he said. 'You and I are going back to the truck near the road block.'

'The truck? Are you crazy?' She was pulling away from him but he was holding her with ease. 'I'm staying with Max.'

Another branch split above their heads.

'This is bad,' Alistair said. 'And it's going to get worse. It's mostly branches and litter flying now, but if it's a real cyclone it'll be trees.'

'But the boys…'

'Help me now,' he said. He'd moved to the edge of the path, where an ancient log lay rotting. 'We push this across.'

'No.'

'Don't be stupid, Georg,' he said. 'Push.'

She stared at him, blind with fear, but his face was implacable.

'Push,' he ordered.

There was no choice. She pushed. Under their combined weight the log slid sideways. 'There'll be a few leaves and stuff falling down,' Alistair yelled to the boys. 'Stand hard against the side, cover your heads with your hands and push your faces against the sides. Right?'

'R-right.' Max sounded terrified but game.

'One more push,' Alistair said, and the thing was done. The log was right over the shaft, anchored by ten feet of wood at either end. As it shifted, the rotten under-edge crumbled a bit more, making it sit flat on the ground.

'No cyclone's going to shift that baby,' Alistair said in satisfaction. 'And it's still strong enough to deflect anything that falls on it. Right, that's the boys safe.' He grabbed a roll of crêpe bandage from his backpack and attached one end to his torch.

'What are you doing?' she whispered.

'Leaving them some light. It's too scary otherwise.' And his torch was pushed through the crack of shaft entry left at the side of the log, and lowered.

'Got it?' he yelled.

'Got it.' Max's cry was more muffled now that the shaft was covered. 'We like the jackets. But Scruffy's whimpering. I reckon his leg's broken. Now I can see…it's bleeding a bit.'

Alistair was at his backpack again. 'Aspirin,' he said. 'Charles is great. Ask and you shall receive.'

He tossed a small blue packet down the shaft.

'Max, give Scruffy a quarter of one of these,'

he yelled. 'Not more. Just a quarter of one and put the rest where he can't get to them. Put it in a chocolate so he'll eat it. Or if he won't, then hold his mouth open, ask your friend to pop it right at the back of his throat and then stroke his throat until he swallows. If his leg keeps bleeding, use the dressing on the torch to bandage his leg. Keep him still and tug the bandage really tight. You can rip the bandage with your teeth if you have to.'

'But you'll be gone.'

'I'm not...' Georgie started, but Alistair caught her to him, held her fast and put a hand over her mouth.

'Yes, we'll be gone, and it might be a few hours before we're back. Max, I have to keep your Georgie safe.'

'I don't want you to go.'

'We don't want to go either,' Alistair called. 'But we need to. You tell each other stories. Eat the chocolate and keep drinking. Make some of the foil round the chocolate into a cup in your hands and give Scruffy a drink. Look after the pup and we'll be back as soon as the storm lessens and it's safe to get you out. OK?'

'Uh, OK.' It wasn't but it had to be.

His face grim, Alistair eased back from the shaft, hauling Georgie with him.

'No,' she sobbed, and he lifted her in his arms and hauled her further back.

'Yes.'

'No!' OK, what he'd said was reasonable but she was beyond reason. Every inch of her being was screaming that to leave Max alone during the storm was crazy. Criminal. Appalling.

The combination of weariness, shock and fear was overwhelming. Crazy or not, she thumped her hands against Alistair and contorted her body, fighting to get away from him.

In answer he simply cradled her tightly against him and started pushing his way back to the creek bed. As if she were a child. A burden of no note.

To fight him was useless. The hysteria of fear finally faded. Alistair didn't speak until she'd stopped fighting him, then he said mildly, 'You're carrying the only torch.' He stumbled a little. 'It'd help if you shone it ahead instead of using it to thump me.'

She was crying, helpless tears of anger and terror. 'Put me down. I'm staying. Please, Alistair, I'm not leaving him. In a cyclone… We don't know how long it'll be. I can't. I can't.'

'I know you can't, which is why I'm carrying you,' he retorted, keeping right on walking. 'Georgie, point the torch.'

'I can't.'

He stumbled. He sighed. He put her down in front of him and held her by the shoulders.

They were far enough from the shaft now for the boys not to hear. He could say what he needed to say.

'Georg, if I thought you'd fit, I would have let you slide down with them,' he said grimly. 'God knows, it looks the safest place anyone can be right now, and the shaft's not horizontal—it's mostly a steep slide rather than a fall. But there really is no room, and I'm not letting you stay up top. What use are you to Max if you're dead?'

'He'll be terrified. I'll just stay. I wouldn't be dead.'

For answer another limb cracked off a tree above their heads.

'You want to bet on it? We go back to the car. It's right next to a fallen tree, the tree's vast and it's protecting the car from the worst of the wind.'

'But if we can't come back... And if the storm's hours...'

'We're much more likely to be alive to come back if we get to safety now.' He'd caught her hand and was tugging her after him. 'If we stay here we'll be dead, and what use is that?'

'Oh, God...'

'I know,' he said more gently. 'You love him.

But love has to make hard choices, Georg, and this is one of them.'

'Love? What do you know about love?'

'I'm just starting to find out,' he said grimly, and kept right on tugging.

CHAPTER EIGHT

BY THE time they got back to the crashed bus the wind had reached the point where speech was almost impossible.

Georgie had ceased to fight. OK, he was right. She knew he was right, but it made it no easier.

At the bus she paused but Alistair shook his head.

'I don't trust those cables,' he said briefly. 'And I'm damned if I want to be in that thing if it hurtles right down to the valley floor.'

Fair enough. He tugged her on, but she was moving with him now, accepting she had no choice. They reached the bikes and used them to get back to the car. That was a hair-raising ride, where they hugged the cliff side of the road to get what shelter they could from the windbreak it formed, avoiding as much as they could of the mountain of debris starting to form on the far side of the road.

Georgie had cause to be thankful they were both wearing full-face helmets. The rain made her almost blind. She needed windscreen wipers, but even if she'd had them, they'd have been useless. They needed their jackets. They were being whipped by debris every inch of the way and her arms were a mass of scratches.

But giving the boys the jackets had been a master stroke of Alistair's, she conceded. It was a comfort to think the little boys were as protected as they could make them.

But finally they reached the truck. Here in the lee made by the combination of the cliff and the massive fallen log, the wind was almost manageable. They wedged their bikes in behind the log, then fought their way against the wind to the back of the truck.

This was a work vehicle. A big four-wheel-drive, with the whole back clear for cargo. There was a blanket tossed into a corner and a crate containing some sort of work gear. Alistair shoved the crate aside and spread the blanket over the bare metal floor.

'Welcome to safety.'

She hadn't realised the full strength of the wind's force—how hard she'd been leaning into the wind. As Alistair tugged her inside she almost fell.

He caught her, steadied her, set her on her knees beside him.

It was too small, she thought, winded, exhausted, shocked. Much too small.

And how long did a cyclone last? They'd radio to find out but, no matter how long it would be, it'd be much too long when Max was stuck out there in the wilderness.

And it'd be too long when she was stuck in the back of a truck with Alistair. He made her feel… He made her feel…

Just cut it out, she told herself breathlessly. She was feeling dizzy and more than a little sick. To find Max and then to be forced to leave him had almost torn her apart.

'I'm running the truck hard against the cliff,' Alistair said. 'That way if it's blasted it can't topple.'

'Can a cyclone really push a truck over?'

'I have no idea but I'm not willing to find out. I want it wedged securely.'

He moved it, blessing Harry for having the forethought to leave the keys in the ignition. Within two minutes he'd backed the truck further toward the cliff so it was edged in a V, with cliff on one side and the fallen tree on the other. Only the front windscreen of the truck was exposed.

There was a cargo screen between the front windscreen and the rear. They should now be safe, even if anything blasted through the windscreen.

How long till the cyclone hit in its full force?
Who knew? She surely didn't.

Max.

Oh, God, she'd go mad.

'Drink,' Alistair said, and handed her a bottle.
'Damn, what we really need is a decent whisky.
Or any whisky. What the hell is this?'

'Glucose-enriched sports drink,' she said. 'To
give us energy. I thought you gave it to the boys.'

'Jill sent us with four bottles. I'm sharing.
Handing over all drinks when we might be stuck
here for twenty-four hours would have been
dumb. And I may be heroic enough to hand over
my jacket and enough chocolate to keep the boys
happy, but all the chocolate would be ludicrous.
So eat some chocolate.' And then as she looked at
the bar with distaste, he unwrapped it and handed
it to her again. 'Eat,' he said, softly but forcibly.
'Last time you ate was at the wedding and you've
been working all night. Eat and then sleep.'

'How can I—?'

'Just do what comes next,' he told her. 'Max
won't thank you for collapsing before we can get
him out. Hell.'

A particularly violent gust was shaking the
truck. Georgie shivered and Alistair tugged her
close.

'Drink your drink and eat your chocolate and don't worry about it,' he said.

'Don't patronise me.'

'I would never do that.'

'You just did.'

'By telling you not to worry?'

'As if I could.'

'I know it's impossible,' he said, his voice softening. 'But they're as safe as we can make them. So we just focus on getting through this next few hours.'

'We shouldn't be here.'

'No,' he said equitably. 'We should be safe back at Croc Creek. But our best chance of retrieving the boys as soon as possible is to stay right here.' He was opening his backpack again, hauling out the radio.

'We should have left the radio with Max,' she said fretfully.

'And if he hadn't been able to use it? We'd have half Croc Creek thinking we were dead. Use your brains, Georg. Let's tell them we're safe.'

'We're not safe.'

'We're as safe as anyone within two hundred miles is right now. Charles?'

Another gust rocked their safe haven. The radio crackled into life. 'Carmichael. Where the hell are you? Carmichael.'

By mutual consent they'd turned off their remaining torch. The batteries should last the night but they had no need of them so why push their luck? If this storm was so bad that they were trapped for longer…

Don't go there.

'We're OK,' Alistair said into the radio transmitter and Charles's sigh of relief was loud enough to be heard over the wind.

'Where the hell have you been?'

'Finding the kids,' Alistair said.

'You've found them?'

'We have. Three of them. There's Max, a dog called Scruffy and another child, a boy of about five.'

'Do we know who he is?'

'We don't know,' Alistair said patiently. 'He doesn't talk.'

'He's hurt?'

'He doesn't seem to be. He's just silent. They both seem OK.'

'So you're on your way in now? How—?'

'We're staying put.' Briefly Alistair outlined the situation. When he finished there was a moment's pause before Charles spoke again.

'You're sure they're safe?' he said at last.

'As safe as we can make them.'

'They'll be terrified.' He paused. 'Well, we can't help that. We're all terrified. In some situations it makes sense to be scared. The full force is coming in now. I was contacting you to say get off the road fast. But you're protected where you are?'

'As protected as we can be.'

'And Georgie's being sensible?'

'Of course.'

'No, of course about it. This is Georgie.'

'I'm being sensible,' Georgie yelled, frustrated and incensed, and Charles's chuckle sounded through the static.

But then the chuckle faded. 'We're in for it,' he said, and his voice was now grim. 'Starting now. You guys stay safe. We can't get to you to help. As of ten minutes ago I ordered everyone inside and no one's moving. I just hope to hell…' He paused. 'OK. Enough. God be with you.'

And the line went dead.

'Um…' Georgie whispered.

'Um?'

'Did Charles just say, "God be with you"?'

'He did.'

'He's never said anything so…personal in his life. I didn't think he knew how.'

'Desperate times call for desperate measures,' Alistair said, and tugged her against him again.

'OK. The way I see it is the worst that can happen to us is the truck goes over. But we're protected— the downed tree will deflect anything else that falls. So we sit and wait it out.'

'I need to go to the bathroom,' she said, and he stilled.

'You don't.'

'I'm a girl. Girls don't have bladders like boys.'

He sighed. 'There's no argument about that one. You want the torch?'

'I'm not going more than four feet from the truck.'

'Very wise.'

'So, yes, I want the torch and I want you to turn your back and close your eyes.'

'Yes, ma'am.'

'Then I'll do the same for you.'

'You're sounding bossy again,' he said, and she switched on the torch in time to see his grin. 'Go ahead. My eyes are closed tight.'

That was the end of laughter. Fifteen minutes later the full force of the cyclone hit. Georgie had been lying in the dark, listening to the wind, thinking of Max, growing more and more fearful.

She was desperately tired but she couldn't sleep. No way. The wind sounded terrifying.

And out there was Max.

She lay rigidly in the dark, willing him to be safe, willing the storm to be not as bad as they feared, willing everything to be OK.

Alistair was right beside her. She was acutely aware of him—too aware of him—and it made things worse. She, who had spent her life fighting to have things under control, was suddenly so far out of her comfort zone that she felt like her world was tilting.

Alistair let her be, seeming to sense she couldn't talk. That she needed to be as far away from him as she could get.

And then she didn't have room to think anything.

She'd thought the wind had been terrifying. With the first blast of the full cyclonic force she was on the other side of the truck and in Alistair's arms and every single scruple was blasted right out of her mind.

She didn't speak. There was no point in speaking. She simply held on for dear life while the wind screamed like the hounds from hell, and the truck rocked back and forth on its axle as if it could take off any minute into the storm.

But it didn't take off. The wind was catching the nose of the truck and shoving it backward, pushing it further into its tight V. Alistair's reasoning had worked. But, still, the force of its rocking was appalling enough. To hell with being alone. To hell with staying in isolation. She buried her face in Alistair's chest and clutched him close.

But who was giving comfort to who? He was holding her as tightly as she held him. There was no choice. In the face of this shared threat there was nothing to do but hold each other, hold and hold…

How long she stayed rigidly fearful, locked against him, she didn't know. The wind didn't lessen and neither did the rocking, but the human body could survive on adrenalin for only so long. The terror that the world would end was fading. But still she stayed where she was. She lay holding tight to Alistair, letting his arms hold her, feeling the beating of his heart against her face. Letting her world settle on a new kind of axis.

Where terrifying was normal.

Where being held by Alistair was normal. Safe.

And something more.

He kissed her hair.

At first she thought she'd imagined it. But, no, she pulled back a little and saw that he was indeed kissing her.

She could see now. There had been no glorious sunrise—the deep black stormclouds made it still almost as dark as night—but not quite. There was sun somewhere behind these stormclouds and there was enough light now to see. It was morning?

And Alistair was smiling. Unbelievably, Alistair was smiling.

'If you've known how long I've wanted to do this,' he murmured against her ear. 'Six months, to be precise. Six long months.'

'You didn't…'

'Georgie, I fell in love with you the moment I saw you.'

'No.'

'No. It's not a good time now to say it,' he agreed, his smile giving way to gravity. 'It's a crazy, dumb time to say it. But I've been lying here feeling like I've never been so afraid in my life, and suddenly I thought that if the wind finally does manage to pick this truck up and transport us to Kansas, I'd never told you. And I've been thinking and thinking, in between worrying about saving our skins, you understand, that I really ought to tell you that I've fallen in love with you.'

She was having trouble breathing, much less speaking. 'You haven't,' she whispered finally, and she wasn't quite sure that she made a sound at all.

'It's too late to say that now,' he said apologetically. 'I'm thinking that I must have fallen in love six months ago. I just never knew I had. I knew you'd attracted me as no other woman had, but I thought it was crazy—that it was just some sexual need.'

'Gee, thanks.'

'See, here's the thing,' he said. 'What I felt then was so strong that when Gina interrupted us that night I could have wept. Afterwards I called myself all sorts of names, but I couldn't figure out how to get rid of how I was feeling.' He was whispering right into her ear. Any further away and she wouldn't be able to hear him. It was the most intimate sort of speech. She should pull away, she thought, but she couldn't. She couldn't.

'And then I walked off the plane two days ago and there you were,' he said. 'Just as I remembered you. And when I carried you away from Max, I felt sick. Because I knew you were torn apart and there wasn't a goddam thing I could do about it, but I would have torn my own heart out to spare you pain. Anyway…' He shifted slightly so he could kiss her, a feather kiss on the tip of her nose—no more—and then moved back so his lips were against her ear again. 'I lay in the dark and it hit me like…well, with the force of a cyclone, that what I'm feeling is this love thing that the world raves about and I've never even believed in. Until now.'

Her heart twisted.

It had been wrenched every which way in the last few hours, she thought, suddenly angry. Love. Terror. Hope.

Love. She loved Max. Her one true thing. They said love could extend to fit all comers. It surely felt like that. The way she felt about this man holding her close was surely something like that. This man she'd thought a manicured wimp in a classy suit, who was suddenly a biker and an abseiler and who'd lifted her as if she weighed nothing.

'Alistair, I always change my mind.' She had to be honest here. He deserved that at least. 'Please, don't fall for me. I'm not…I don't even trust myself.'

'Why not?' Maybe they were getting accustomed to the wind. Or maybe it was that they were so close to each other. They'd relaxed a little now, lying face to face, their mouths barely inches apart. Their noses were practically touching. The most intimate of settings…

'I fall for the violent ones,' she whispered. 'Like my dad. Like Ron. And I can't…do anything about it.'

'So you're saying you can't fall for me.'

'Yes, but that's just the problem.' She barely understood this herself—how to explain it to him? 'I have fallen for you. You said you felt this… thing. Well, I do, too, but I don't trust myself. How can I trust you?'

'How can you not?'

'See, if I fall for you, I don't know how you'll be,' she said, and she knew she was sounding pathetic but she didn't have a choice. 'And if you ever hit Max…'

'I would never hit Max,' he said, astounded. 'And what about if I ever hit you? Georgie, do you think I could do that?'

'No.' But she bit her lip and shook her head. 'Yes. I don't know. You see, all my values— they're all over the place. I can't figure out how to trust anyone because whenever I do it's all wrong. I came to Crocodile Creek to get away from stuff…'

'To get away from someone?'

'From a whole string of someones,' she said desperately. 'Guys I thought might be the one, only every time I did they just…they just…'

'Hit you?'

'I'd never let them,' she said with an attempt at dignity. What was it about this place, this situation, that was letting her expose herself so completely? 'Do you really think I'd let anyone hit me?'

'Only Smiley,' he said, smiling softly into her eyes. 'Only if it was absolutely necessary to put someone in jail.'

'I'm good at defending myself,' she said. 'I've had to be. But if you were great to me...'

'You'd think I was soft?' He was trying desperately to understand, she thought, and it made it worse.

'I can't figure it out myself.'

'You don't think you could give it a chance? Let me into your life a little and take it a step at a time?'

'You're leaving straight after Cal and Gina's wedding.'

'See, here's the thing,' he said, almost apologetically. 'Charles has offered me a job.'

She felt like her breath had been punched out of her. A particularly violent blast rocked the truck, but she was getting more fearful of what was happening right in here.

'You'll never do it.'

'Would you hate it?'

'I... It's nothing to do with me.'

'If I stayed, would you run again?'

'I can't,' she said, and her voice was a wail. 'I

have Max. Max has all these friends. Gina's little boy, CJ. Charles's adopted daughter, Lily. Mrs Grubb. They all love Max to bits and he loves them. How could I walk away?'

'But you're so fearful of me that you might?'

'I don't know,' she whispered.

Another crash. Something hard and solid crashed down on the top of the truck. She shivered and Alistair was holding her tight again.

She should fight him. She should...

She couldn't.

'One day at a time,' he said, whispering against her ear. 'Let's just do it like that. I know I've added to the pressure—I shouldn't have told you but, you know, I thought maybe this might be the only chance I ever have to say it so, damn, I'm going to say it. Georgie, like it or not, take it or leave it, I've suddenly figured it out. I love you. And unless you object very, very loudly, so loudly that I can hear you above this damned cyclone, I intend to kiss you into the middle of next week. Right here. Right now. Any objections?'

Any objections?

Of course she had objections. She had a thousand objections. She just couldn't quite manage to voice them. She just couldn't quite manage...

He kissed her.

CHAPTER NINE

THE eye of the storm, when it came, came so swiftly that for a moment Georgie thought she was dreaming.

She'd been fast asleep. Wise or not, dopy or not, she'd been sleeping in Alistair's arms. The blast of the wind had been dulled by the beat of his heart. His declaration had been crazy. It had frightened her. But she'd been honest, she told herself. He knew where he stood.

So when he'd kissed her, what was a girl to do but respond? What was a girl to do but take comfort where comfort was offered?

What was a girl to do but to savour every single moment of his kisses? Of this time she'd held him tightly. Before the world had blasted its dreadful reality back against her.

So she'd gone to sleep, and maybe he had, too. She woke up feeling warm and safe and cherished. And the wind had stopped.

She opened one eye and then the other.

'Alistair.'

'I'm hearing it,' he said, and she could feel the rumble of his voice as well as hear it. Nice.

Very nice.

'The eye of the cyclone,' he said.

'You mean it'll come back.'

'Yeah, but we may have time.' He set her away from him, but then he smiled, tugged her back and kissed her, briefly but hard on the lips. A man claiming his own.

'Let's see,' he said, and reached for the radio.

Charles answered in seconds.

'You guys are safe?'

'We're safe,' Alistair snapped. He was hauling the box of gear forward to inspect its contents. Georgie moved to help him. He talked into the radio while she tugged open the lid.

'It's hell here,' Charles said, 'but the hospital's still standing.'

'As bad as that?'

'Maybe worse,' Charles said grimly. 'I can't spare anyone to help you.'

'You don't need to.' Alistair had discovered a coil of rope. He ran his hand along its length. Twenty feet? Maybe a little more. 'We have everything we need.'

'But the kids…'

'We'll get them out now.'

'You have maybe an hour, tops,' Charles snapped. 'Don't take any risks.'

'We won't take any more risks than we need to,' Alistair said gently. 'But even by being in the hospital back at Crocodile Creek we'd be taking risks. The guys are saying the eye might give us an hour's break?'

'That's the outer estimate.'

'Then we need to move,' Alistair said, and he replaced the radio in the backpack and hauled open the truck doors. To chaos.

The rainforest was a tangle of smashed timber, debris flung everywhere, the remains of trees mixed with the broken shards of others. It was like a huge crazy game of pick-up sticks.

The silence was eerie.

They hardly talked as they hauled the bikes out from their cover. They'd pushed them almost completely under the fallen tree, and the wind had pushed them further. But they were essentially undamaged.

Could they ride them? Maybe, in the lee of the cliff.

'We'll try,' Alistair said. They'd never get back to the mine shaft without them. Not in time.

And somehow they did. It was a feat of pure

riding skill, Georgie thought, but it wasn't her skill. Alistair rode first, and she merely placed her bike's wheels in the tracks made by his.

Even so, it was a ghastly ride, with them half pushing, half riding through a mass of tangled undergrowth, a crazy jumble of smashed forest. The lee of the cliff had deflected some of the mess but not all, and it hadn't deflected water. Their wheels were sliding in pure slush. How much rain had there been? A flood? At times the road was more like a river, and there was nothing for it but to get off and push through.

But somehow they did, with Alistair's fierce determination to push through more than matching her own. As they reached the crash site and came to a halt, she felt like her insides had been put in a mouli mix.

There was still no wind. Not a breath, and it was still almost dark.

Ominous was too good a word for the sensation she was feeling, and she'd gone past terror. But fear had to be put aside. What they were attempting might seem crazy, but the alternative was to leave the kids in the shaft longer. And the land was now waterlogged. If there was another slip…

Don't think about it. Just think about putting the next step in front of the last. Alistair was off his bike, fighting his way through broken branches to the edge of the road. She fought her way through to join him and stared down.

The bus was no longer there.

For a moment she thought she was dreaming. The cables holding the trees hadn't snapped, but the trees to which they'd been attached were no longer there either.

The bus had presented a vast mass of metal, its broken windows opening it to the elements. The result must have been inevitable.

And she'd wanted to shelter in it?

'Oh, God,' she whispered, and Alistair's hand caught hers. He gripped, hard.

'Come on. We have work to do.'

Max. Please, God, Max.

It was lucky they had the old creek bed to follow, otherwise they'd never have found them. This was no simple walk, as it had been only hours ago. It was a mass of tangled timber they had to climb through, clamber over, creep under. And the creek bed was now just that—a torrent of tumbling water.

'The time,' Alistair murmured, and she glanced at her watch. Twenty-five minutes since the silence had started. They had an hour at most before the force started again. Oh, God.

She stumbled and Alistair caught her and steadied her yet again.

'We can't go any faster than we're going,' he said. 'Come on.'

At least he wasn't suggesting they go back. And, Georgie thought, that's huge. This wasn't Alistair's little brother stuck in the shaft. Alistair had had every right to stay back in Crocodile Creek. Right now, the sensible thing to do to protect himself was to stay in the truck and wait for the second blast to finish.

But that might be another half a day and he'd know—he'd know!—that she couldn't bear it. That running for safety even for those first hours had almost killed her.

He was doing this for her and she felt sick.

'I had no right,' she said, and he glanced across at her in concern. He'd managed to get over a half-rotten tree trunk, and he was helping her over.

'Sorry?'

'I had no right to drag you into this,' she said, louder this time and more strongly.

And, unexpectedly, astonishingly he chuckled.

'See, that's just it,' he said. 'What we were talking about. This love thing. You'd better get used to it. I love you, Georgie Turner, and from now on you don't drag me anywhere. From now on, you'll just look behind and I'll be following.'

It was such a huge statement it took her breath away. She didn't… She couldn't…

'Don't get your knickers in a twist,' he said, and he grinned still more. 'We go down together, Georgie, or we don't go down at all. How romantic's that? But if you don't mind, I prefer the latter option so we need to move ourselves quite sharply.'

She gulped. She swallowed. He grabbed her hand still more tightly and led her forward.

Once again, if they hadn't known exactly where to go, they'd have been lost. The landscape was so different it was weird. The rainforest canopy had been swept to the forest floor. There were mountains of litter. Mountains.

But somehow they kept to the track. Somehow. And then…

'Here,' Alistair said. 'This log.' And then he raised his voice.

'Max.'

There was a moment's deathly silence when Georgie's heart forgot to beat. Then, magically, wondrously from below them…'Georgie?' The yell broke in the middle into a sob, and Georgie thought her own heart would break. But this was no time for emotion.

'I'm here,' she yelled back. 'We promised we'd come. Max, are you OK?'

'J-just scared. It was so noisy. We weren't game to use our torch much in case it conked out. And there's water in here now, right up to our knees. Can you get us out now?'

Water. Oh, God.

'Sure.' Or she thought they could. She hoped they could. Alistair seemed to know what he was doing. He was looping the rope he'd brought around a vast tree trunk that had crashed right by the shaft.

Rising water.

It didn't bear thinking of.

'How's the other little boy?' she asked.

'He still won't talk. He's cuddling Scruffy.'

'Is Scruffy his dog?'

'Scruffy's my dog.'

'Why aren't you cuddling him?' she asked, trying to figure things out.

'My arm's sore.'

Her heart stilled all over again. 'Has it been bleeding?'

'A bit of stuff came down just after you left,' he said. 'It hit me. But the kid bandaged me up with some of the bandage you tied on the torch.'

'So he bandaged you with the same bandage you used on Scruffy's leg?' Alistair was knotting his rope, forming a loop in the end.

'The kid tore it with his teeth,' Max said. 'I was… I was crying.'

'Oh, Max…' And who was this strange kid? She wanted to hug him.

Why was she up here?

'Are you coming down now?' Max obviously felt the same way she did.

'Alistair is,' she said, as Alistair slid the looped end of the rope into the shaft.

'No,' Alistair said. 'You are.'

'Me.'

'You can't pull me out but I can pull you out,' he said. 'It makes sense. And if I go down and get stuck, I can't see you sensibly going back to the truck and waiting again.'

'I…I would.' Maybe.

'I'm not risking it,' he said. 'Put your foot in the loop. See the knots? They're to hang onto—they'll give you a better grip as I lower you. You go down and we'll figure out who comes up first when you're down there. Just hang onto it, relax and I'll pull.'

'You can't.'

'Watch me.'

She trusted him. There was nothing else to do. She put her foot into the loop and slid over the side.

The kids at the base were shining their torch up.

'Lean against the far side of the shaft and put your faces against the wall again,' Alistair warned them. 'There'll be rubble falling.'

She was on her way down. He was lowering her with the ease of a mechanical lift, as if such a weight was no problem at all.

But then she forgot about Alistair as she reached the base and Max was in her arms. He was wet and cold and shivery and he clung to her fiercely. Her Max.

It was such a tight fit. There was no room for them all, but Max was huddled into her, sobbing, and her arms enveloped him and then because there was no room and there was a need here as well, she was enveloping the other kid as well, and the dog…

The dog was licking her face.

'Move,' Alistair said above them. He was shining his torch down and his voice sounded a bit wobbly. 'Come on, Georg. I know this is a reunion but every second counts. Hugs are for when we're safe.'

Right. She gulped and pulled away a little.

'Littlest first,' she said. 'Can you hold onto the rope?' she asked the small boy.

He nodded.

'Will you tell me your name?'

Silence.

'He could hold Scruffy 'cos he's the lightest,' Max volunteered, and they all looked at Scruffy and then the silent child reached out and took him and held him. Tight.

It was a big ask for a little boy to put his foot in the loop, to hold Scruffy in one arm and the rope in the other, but there was that silent look of determination about him that told Georgie he could do it.

She smiled at him, gave him another swift hug for good measure and sent him on his way.

One boy and one dog rose smoothly to the surface.

The rope came down again. 'Max's turn,' Alistair said from above them.

'Georgie,' Max said, and gulped back a sob. But there was no time for hesitation.

'Go,' she said, and pushed him upward, then waited in the dark shaft for the rope to return. She was standing calf-deep in water, but at least her leathers and biker boots were keeping her dry.

The boys had been soaked. To have been stuck down there for hours... It didn't bear thinking of.

But there was no time to think. A moment later the rope was lowered again. Alistair tugged her up as if she weighed nothing. She rose smoothly into daylight, and Max and the kid and the dog and Alistair were all waiting for her. They grasped her under the arms as she came over the side and she wasn't sure who was doing the pulling.

But she was safe and here it came. The hug. Ten seconds of pure group hug—the whole lot of them. She felt so overwhelmed she couldn't do anything but hold and hold and hold.

'Right,' Alistair said, in a voice thick with an emotion he couldn't conceal. 'Enough emotion. We have a cyclone to outrun.' He turned the little boy to face him—their nameless child. 'You'll come with us?'

The little boy nodded, but Georgie thought it was great that Alistair had asked.

'What's your name?' she asked him again. He looked like a little owl, freckly and wiry and filthy, and, oh, so serious. 'You've been so brave. Can you tell us who you are?'

Nothing.

'Well, let's call you Rowdy,' Alistair said, and gave the kid another swift hug. Man to man. 'It's a man's name because you've just been as brave as a man.'

'Why did you choose Rowdy?' Max asked.

''Cos he's the rowdiest man I know,' Alistair said. 'Rowdy means really, really noisy. All this noise… I don't know how we stand it.' He chuckled and suddenly they were all smiling. 'So, Rowdy, will you come with us?'

Another nod. And another small smile.

'Great,' Alistair said. 'But you're taking a ride. On my back, Rowdy, mate.' He tugged his backpack around to his front and swung the little boy onto his back. The child was wearing only one shoe, and under the grime of a filthy, wet sock they could see a smudge of bloodstain. 'Georg, can you carry Scruffy?'

'Of course I can,' she said. She picked up the little dog, she grabbed Max's hand—and they ran.

Or they clambered. They moved as fast as they could over the rough terrain.

By the time they reached the road the wind was building up again. It was whistling eerily through the trees. The trees were starting to moan.

Please, please, please, Georgie thought. They had to get back to the truck. They must. She knew what the force was like now and she knew that Alistair was right. To be out here with no protection meant death.

They'd reached the bikes. Alistair didn't hesitate. By the time Georgie had pulled her bike to point back towards the truck he was on his bike, Rowdy was in front of him and he was holding his hands out for the dog.

'You can't,' she said, and he grimaced and motioned to his backpack.

'I took everything out. The dog goes in.'

'He won't,' Georgie breathed.

'He does or he'll stay here,' he said grimly, and before she could protest again he'd slipped the little dog inside. As if he knew exactly what was expected, the dog hunkered down so only his nose was sticking out. Alistair grinned and slung the pack carefully over his shoulders.

'We're all being sensible here,' he told Georgie. 'Max goes behind you. Go.'

How they made it she'd never know. It was hard enough for her to have Max behind her. Dirt bikes weren't meant for passengers. But Alistair hadn't been able to put Rowdy behind him because of Scruffy in the backpack. So Rowdy was huddled against his chest.

The set-up on his bike looked somehow... heart-wrenching? The wind was really rising now and Georgie had to concentrate fiercely as they pushed on, but there was still a part of her that was far too aware of Alistair Carmichael.

This man was about as different as it was possible to be from the slick, professional doctor she'd met from the plane two days ago.

He hadn't shaved for at least twenty-four hours. He was wearing borrowed leather pants, a ripped shirt and an ancient helmet, battered and filthy. *He* was battered and filthy.

He had a kid cradled against his breast and a dog in a backpack. He'd won Rowdy's trust with instinctive ease. He was riding a mud-splattered dirt bike with skill and precision.

He was heart-meltingly, life-changingly gorgeous.

He'd been offered a job in Croc Creek.

Life-changing? Could she change her life for him?

Now was no time for decisions. She slowed as he did, ducking and weaving around timber felled by the storm. Max was holding on for dear life behind her. She was aware that he was holding her tighter with the right arm than the left. What was the damage?

She should stop and look, only the blasts of wind were terrifying on their own now. To stop except for the times when she had to get off and shove her bike through water or around some obstacle was suicide. She'd fallen twenty feet behind Alistair's bike as it was.

There was a massive crack of splintering timber from above her head. She slammed her brakes and stopped inches from the trunk of a falling forest giant. For one heart-stopping moment she thought Alistair and his precious cargo were underneath. Oh, God… But then, almost before the last of the branches had sighed and settled, there was a hoarse shout, so loud it could be heard above the wind.

'Georg…'

There was such fear there that she caught her breath. Alistair was afraid. For her?

And she'd felt the same, she thought, dumping her bike and gathering Max tight against her. The little boy had come to the end of his resources. He was a mass of trembling fear, sobbing against her, hugging her close.

She gathered him tightly against her and hugged, but she had to yell back.

'Alistair.'

'Georg.' It was a shout of near relief—almost relief but still there was fear.

'It missed us,' she yelled. She'd been daydreaming, she thought. As fearful as this situation was, she'd allowed her attention to stray a little. She'd fallen back a little behind Alistair.

That moment's inattention had saved her life.

The mound of fallen timber in front of her was massive, but the wind was already shifting it again. She had to get over…

Max was going nowhere. His feet had gone from under him. 'We have to go beneath and around,' she told him, but he was incapable of moving.

'Max…'

She couldn't carry him. She couldn't…

'Georg…' How he'd got there so fast she didn't know, but Alistair was there. He'd gone down the hill from the road and clambered around, underneath the roots of the fallen tree. There was a trickle of blood slipping down his cheek. His face was white and shocked. He reached them and gathered them hard against him, and swore. And swore and swore.

'Max can't walk,' she told him, taking strength from the sheer bulk of him.

'Of course not.' He swung Max into his arms. 'Max, you're a hero,' he told the little boy. 'But you've done enough. The rest is up to me.'

As it was. Max may have run out of resources but Georgie was a close second. She followed numbly as Alistair retraced his steps but she was aware that he had to slow his steps not to draw ahead. It took them three times as long as he'd taken to get around the uprooted stump.

But finally they made it. Rowdy and Scruffy were huddled where they'd been put—right underneath the mound of fallen branches, with the bike shoved in after them to protect them from the worst of the blast.

The wind was so fierce now that it was an effort to move at all. Left to her own resources, Georgie might have stayed where she was. She'd have had to—there was no way Max was moving.

But Alistair was made of sterner stuff.

'Move,' he said. 'We ditch the bikes here but I'm thinking we're only minutes from the truck. Georgie, can you carry Rowdy?'

She took a deep breath. 'Of course I can.'

'Of course you can,' he said, and he smiled. 'My Georgie.'

And they did. Ten minutes later, battered beyond belief but essentially still in one piece, they reached the truck.

It was still as they'd left it, wedged firmly between cliff and tree.

It was all Georgie could do not to kiss it.

The windscreen was smashed. A branch had hit it, piercing it, but, instead of leaving it open to the elements, more foliage had been blasted against the front, making it a rigid shelter that nothing could now reach.

Including them. It took Alistair five minutes to pull enough of the rubbish away for them to enter. Georgie couldn't help—she sat and cradled two terrified children to her until he'd cleared the path in. He hoisted his backpack in first—with dog— and then motioned for them to precede him.

They were home.

She climbed in, tugging the kids in after her.

Alistair climbed in and pulled the doors behind him.

Safe.

The word was so overwhelming it was all she could do not to sob. But Max was already sobbing and Rowdy was so white she thought he might pass out. And the dog had crawled out of its backpack and was cringing, its belly flat on the floor, its eyes huge, its tail flattened. Georgie couldn't bear it. She lifted the pup into her arms first and then tugged Max against her, and then Rowdy looked so terrified as well that she tried to fit him against her as well, but it didn't work.

Or it did work.

Because Alistair had gathered the child against him and he was holding Scruffy and Max as well, and maybe a bit of her, too.

A sandwich squeeze. Five of them taking comfort, giving comfort, not able to speak for the moment—not a able to do anything except hug and realise that they were alive and that there just might be an afterwards.

The second blast of the cyclone was worse than the first but it couldn't reach them.

For the first hour they hardly moved. This was no time for assessment. It was simply time for reassurance and comfort and holding.

But then, as the little boys grew used to the rocking of the van, as they accustomed themselves to the screech of wind against the metal, they ate a few more of the chocolate bars that were still miraculously in Georgie's pack and the children drifted toward sleep.

They couldn't have slept at all in the long hours down the shaft, Georgie thought. It must have been a special kind of hell.

The boys needed to be examined, but for now comfort was of paramount importance, even for the little dog. He'd included himself in their sandwich squeeze and they were pleased to have him. Georgie and Alistair lay on either side of the kids and the dog, but they weren't rigidly side by side. The kids were sprawled over them like a litter of puppies, and so was Scruffy.

'Yeah, I love you, too,' Alistair told him as the little dog gave him a slurpy kiss and Max even gave a sleepy giggle.

Even Rowdy smiled a little.

What was it with the child?

'There doesn't seem to be a physical reason why he's not talking,' Alistair murmured as both children relaxed even further into heavy sleep. 'I thought at first he must be deaf, but he was responding to my directions on the bike.'

'Max says he hasn't said a word.'

'I did a fast check of his mouth as he came out of the shaft,' Alistair said. 'No damage.' He stirred, seemingly reluctant to break their hold. 'We need to check them completely.'

Which they did—sort of, though not so comprehensively that they'd wake them. Max had a long, ugly scratch on his arm. It had bled through the dressings Rowdy had put on, but when Georgie carefully unwrapped it she thought it didn't need stitches.

'And cleaning can wait until we're out of here,' Alistair said. 'We'll give him a dose of antibiotic but I'm not waking him for germs.'

Rowdy had got off even more lightly. A few scratches and bruises, with a couple of deeper scratches on his foot. He'd been wearing only one shoe. They tugged both the kids' shoes and socks off, getting rid of water that might well be contaminated. Weren't gold mines full of stuff you didn't want to think about?

They couldn't worry about that now. Rowdy seemed fine. He was huddled against Max, supremely trusting. The little boy's pockets were still stuffed with the chocolate bars they'd tossed into the shaft, and as she tried to remove them he whimpered and clutched at them as if they were important. But he wasn't still hungry. What was his story?

Georgie thought back to the bus passengers she'd seen. Who had been with this kid? No one who'd been capable of missing him, obviously.

One of the DOAs?

'Don't think about it,' Alistair growled, and she looked across at him and grimaced. This man could read her thoughts. It was a really scary ability.

'We need to make a splint.' He'd unwrapped Scruffy's back leg. This was a wound that needed proper medical attention. 'How's your animal husbandry?'

'Lousy,' she said.

'Mine, too. But this leg's fractured. Hell, he must have dragged himself over those stones, running away. Poor little rat.'

'Yes.'

'Will you let Max keep him?'

'Of course I will.' Some things were no-brainers.

He grinned. 'There you go. Georgie of the huge heart, expanding to fit all comers. Bear me in mind when you're working out how far you have to stretch.'

'Alistair…'

'I know,' he said, and he smiled at her with a look of such tenderness that she almost gasped. 'Much too soon. But inevitable, my Georg. Let's just work on it as a given.'

CHAPTER TEN

EVEN when the cyclone was past, their ordeal wasn't over. The cyclone had torn apart the district, wreaked its havoc and then swept out to sea, but there it paused and hovered, threatening still and keeping the land buffeted by gale-force winds.

There was no single moment when they thought, Now it's over, now its safe.

But as the worst of the wind died, the water damage made itself felt. The road where the truck was parked slipped a little and the truck lurched sideways. Not very much, but enough to force their decision to search for another place to shelter.

Georgie knew the area. Dan Mackers's banana plantation was the closest. Dan had evacuated himself and his family as they'd brought out the bus-crash victims, but surely somewhere there they could find refuge. The Mackerses' main house was up past the bus-crash site, but there were a couple of smaller huts used for itinerant workers that were closer to where they were. Georgie had delivered the Mackerses' children and she'd been to several Mackers parties. She knew where the huts were—or she hoped she did.

It was now impossible to use the bikes. Carrying Rowdy and Scruffy and helping Max all they could, they fought their way on foot through the mess that was the road and found one of the cottages still standing. Almost. Its outhouse had disappeared, but who needed outhouses?

The roof was intact, the place was dry and, best yet, there was bedding, canned provisions and bottled water.

'And mashed bananas for as far as the eye can see,' Alistair said in satisfaction.

They were safe, but they were stuck. There was no telephone—all lines were long down. In that last mad dash, taking the boys back to the truck, Alistair had transferred his radio from his backpack to his pocket. Somehow his whole pocket had been torn away, and the radio had been lost.

Charles would be frantic, Georgie thought as the hours wore on, but then she thought, No, he'd guess, or at least he'd hope. The weather was too wild for anyone to institute a search.

They settled down to wait.

They treated the boys' needs properly. They

stripped them of their wet clothes, cuddled them and told them silly stories. They resplinted Scruffy's leg and kept him dry and warm and still.

They slept.

There were only two single beds in the hut. The boys and Scruffy had one. Alistair and George shared the other. No impropriety—how could there be in such close proximity to the boys?—but Alistair hugged her to sleep and there was no way she was objecting. No way at all.

He felt so right. Could she make room in her life for him? she found herself wondering. Could she learn to trust?

She didn't know, but more and more she knew she had to try.

And then, at midday on the day after the storm, the chopper came sweeping in from the east. First it headed for the main Mackers place—the obvious place to search. It hovered overhead for maybe twenty minutes as those in it obviously searched unsuccessfully for a place to land, and Alistair and Georgie fretted impotently and wondered whether they could make a fire with saturated green wood and no matches.

But then those on the helicopter obviously decided to give up and fly instead to check the outer huts.

There was no need for the helicopter to hover and search here, for they were out of the hut, waving and shouting, the little boys yelling louder than they were, and Georgie thought she was probably crying but, hell, who was watching?

Cal was at the controls. And Mike was up there, too. Mike, who must be having the most tumultuous introduction to married life anyone could imagine. And Harry. Her friends.

They were yelling and cheering and Georgie and the kids were yelling and cheering, too, but Georgie had tears running down her face she couldn't stop. Alistair's arm came round her waist and he gripped hard.

'I don't have a handkerchief any more,' he said, and she choked on a chuckle. And she didn't move away from his embrace.

It didn't matter what the guys on the chopper thought. She'd worry about that tomorrow.

There was no place to land. They'd have to be retrieved by harness but that was fine by all of them. The little boys had recovered enough to be brave—even excited at such a form of rescue. Harry lowered himself down in the harness for the first retrieval and Georgie let go of Alistair and ran forward and hugged Harry.

For the normally emotionally contained Georgie

this was well out of character, and she could see Harry's astonishment.

'Hey,' he said, and hugged her back. Then he turned to Alistair and held out his hand. 'And hey to you, too. All of you. You're all safe?'

'We're all safe.' Georgie was struggling to get her voice to work. 'You know Max,' she managed. 'And this is Rowdy. Scruffy's inside with a broken leg.'

'Scruffy?'

'Max's dog,' Georgie said, and grabbed Max's hand. 'Our dog.'

'Max,' Harry said, and shook his hand. 'And Rowdy.' Alistair had his hand on Rowdy's shoulder. Rowdy was pressing hard against Alistair—a small boy in a big unknown world. But he was brave. Harry shook Rowdy's small hand and Rowdy gave him a small smile. 'You have no idea how much Charles has been sweating on you guys,' Harry said, still smiling down at Rowdy. 'What happened to your radio?'

'They should make those damned things windproof,' Alistair said. 'Can you take us home?'

'That's what we're here for,' Harry said, and proceeded to do just that.

And twenty minutes later they were in the air. Alistair, Georgie and their brood were safely tucked in the rear of the helicopter, but they could see down to the cyclone-ravaged land.

The damage had been appalling. It was still appalling. By the time they landed Georgie was so overwhelmed she could hardly speak.

Whole forests had been flattened like matchsticks. Plantations destroyed. Buildings were simply no longer there. The swollen river was crammed with debris.

'How many dead?' she asked as they landed and Harry and Mike helped them out.

'Ten that we know of,' Harry said soberly. 'That's including the bus-crash victims. But there's lots of places we haven't checked yet.'

'Oh, Harry…'

'At least you guys are safe,' he said, and turned to take Rowdy as Alistair lifted him from the plane. 'We were all going nuts.'

And, giving truth to his statement, here came Gina. She'd been on the veranda of the doctors' house—one of the few buildings not obviously damaged. She'd shielded her eyes from the sun as the chopper had landed, seemingly hoping against hope that it was…

And it was. She squealed her delight and came tearing across the intervening ground as if she was running for her life. Yelling.

'They're back. Our Georgie's back. And our Max and our Alistair. And there's new guys. They're back. They're safe back home.'

And before Alistair found himself enveloped in a bear hug that practically knocked him off his feet, he had the forethought to steady himself by hanging onto Georgie.

Our Georgie. Our Max. Our Alistair. And there's new guys.

It felt like a family, Alistair thought, and he pulled back to check that Rowdy wasn't too overwhelmed.

A family.

It felt really good.

He just had to get Georgie to agree.

A family.

The fuss was almost over.

Well, hardly. There was still the huge clean-up that had hardly started as yet, but for tonight Georgie could lie in her own bed and think about what had happened to her. Max was right by her side, and Rowdy was on the other side of her. Scruffy was in a basket under her bed.

Her world had expanded. They still didn't have a clue as to who Rowdy was, but that could wait.

If no one claimed him, maybe she would, she thought dreamily. Mum to two kids and a dog?

It sounded great.

And Alistair?

He'd let her be. They'd separated to have glorious hot showers—the water supply here was fantastic. Alistair had been needed in the hospital—Megan and the patient he'd operated on from the bus crash both needed his care. He'd been accepted as one of the Croc Creek doctors. Everyone was treating him as one of them.

Except her.

He loved her.

She just had to trust.

It was such a big thing. Huge. She couldn't even explain it to herself.

She loved him. Or she thought she loved him. If he left right now she'd break her heart.

So throw your heart in the ring. Take the plunge.

'It's Max, too,' she whispered, hugging her little brother close. 'To entrust Max…'

She could.

Head and heart were warring. How could she trust?

Max muttered a little and moved away a bit. It was muggy, close, and her cuddling was making him sticky.

She was cuddling him for her, not for him.

She let him move away a little and felt a stab of loss.

Oh, for heaven's sake, go to sleep. Go to sleep!

She couldn't. She stared up into the dark for a long time.

There were sounds on the veranda. Footsteps. Someone else wasn't sleeping. One of the other doctors?

Alistair? His bedroom was right next door. Maybe…

Maybe she'd be dumb to find out.

But the thought was irresistible. Carefully she slid out of bed, inching out so quietly that even Scruffy in his basket under the bed didn't stir.

She lifted the latch and walked out into the moonlight, turning and carefully latching the door after her. If Alistair was here…she'd want to be able to talk. She'd want to be able to…

She turned, smiling already at the thought.

'You,' a voice said, and she froze.

Smiley.

He was right in front of her. Maybe he'd been checking the rooms, maybe searching for her. Before she could react he'd moved with lightning speed, grabbing her, hauling her around and shoving his hand tightly across her mouth.

'Bitch,' he said, and her head swam.

She could fight. She'd been trained to fight. But he'd moved too fast, shoving her down hard on the ancient settee, seizing her arms and dragging them up behind her.

'You make one sound and I'll kill you, and then I'll go in and kill that kid,' he said. 'I swear. Yeah, I'll go to jail but I'm going to jail anyway. Maybe ten years, they're saying. Well, what's a few more years added to ten? If I'm going to spend time inside then every minute I'm in there I'm going to think how much I hurt you.' He'd twisted something around her wrists—some sort of length of rubber. He twisted so hard she cried out involuntarily, and he grabbed her hair and hauled at it.

'I told you. One more sound and I kill you now. I could break your neck just like that. Maybe I will. Or I have a knife. Hmm, what will I use? But that's not for here, and if you scream now the kid gets it as well as you.' And he tugged her to her feet.

She was helpless. He had her by the hair with one hand, the other he was using to tighten the bands at her wrists and push her toward the stairs.

'Georgie…'

Oh, God, it was Max. Max… No!

'Georgie…' His tiny body launched at Smiley as if he were a missile. 'Georgie…'

Smiley released her hair and struck Max, hard. The crash of his fist made a dull, sick sound and Max crumpled on the steps.

'You bastard...'

Alistair launched himself out of the darkness with such ferocity she didn't at first know it was him. Smiley's fist had crunched into Max with force but it was nothing to the force Alistair used. One moment Georgie was being held by the wrists, the next Smiley was hit so hard that he was propelled right over the balustrade into the garden below.

Alistair was over, too, launching himself at Smiley with unbelievable force.

'He has a knife,' she screamed, and there was another sickening crunch.

'Not any more he doesn't,' Alistair breathed, and then grunted as Smiley obviously made contact with him.

'Help.' Georgie's lungs were right there. Her only weapon. Unable to be used when Max had been attacked, she used them to full effect now. 'Help.' But she was huddled over Max. 'Max...' Dear God, he was so still...

Lights were going on inside. 'Help,' she screamed again, for good measure, and the veranda lights flooded on. She could see...

Max was conscious. He was stunned. A trickle of blood oozed from just beside his ear but he was looking up at her, wondering…

She wanted to hold him close but couldn't because her hands were still tied. Then she remembered—Alistair… She hauled herself up.

He had Smiley. Somehow Alistair had him tight, hauling him to his feet, swearing…

'You…'

Smiley's foot smashed down onto Alistair's, crunching so hard Georgie could feel his pain.

People were spilling out onto the veranda. Gina. Luke. Rowdy. Oh, Rowdy…

She turned back to Alistair. She felt his fury. Thump him, she thought, screaming in her head. Thump him back.

But he didn't. He gripped Smiley's arms so tightly that Smiley couldn't move, and he propelled him forward into the solid base of the veranda.

'Come and take him before I kill him,' he said to his friends. He wrenched Smiley forcibly against the balustrade. 'If I do what I really want, I'm done for. There's no way I'm letting this scumball say I used undue force.'

He stood motionless, holding Smiley in a grip of iron until Cal got himself together, and Luke, and suddenly Harry was there, too—where had he come from? All she knew was that Smiley was immobilised.

She turned back to Max, and Alistair was by her side, releasing her hands then holding her tight, looking down at Max with eyes that were as fearful as her own.

'Max…' His voice shook.

'I'm OK,' Max said, and his voice wobbled. 'He just punched me.'

'W-we're used to it,' Georgie said, turning to hold Max.

'Well, get unused to it,' Alistair growled, and his voice wobbled a bit more. But then it firmed, and strengthened, 'No more. That's it. You guys have been punched for the last time. I swear to you… Georgie, I want to marry you but even if you won't, I swear I'll stick around and make sure that no one touches you again. I swear. The violence ends. Right here. Right now.'

The violence ends. Right here. Right now.

She looked up at him with eyes that were bright with unshed tears. What had he said? *I want to marry you…*

It was enough. The trust started right then and there.

How to fall in love with someone because they hadn't hit out?

Alistair had hit with a force she couldn't believe. He'd used violence to protect his own. But then it was finished.

Smiley had hit him. And she'd felt that crunch on Alistair's bare foot. He was wearing boxer shorts and nothing else. How could he ever have thought he'd win against Smiley?

But he had won—not only with force but also with lack of force.

Her Alistair.

Soon she'd check out his foot. Soon she'd attend to the bruise already swelling on Max's face.

But for now…

'You'll stick around?' she whispered.

'Yes.'

She swallowed and hugged Max some more. 'Max, what do you think of me and you and Alistair being a family?'

And then she thought…family. Max. Maybe Alistair hadn't factored that into the equation.

But it seemed he had. He was gathering her into his arms, and because she was holding Max he was gathering him in, too. And then Rowdy, white-faced and obviously terrified, was limping down the steps, and Scruffy was clunking down on his splint, too. They were all gathered in as well.

'Welcome all comers,' Alistair said, in a voice Georgie failed to recognise. 'I once thought I wanted control. I even once thought isolation was the way to go. I must have been mad. Georgie Turner, biker, obstetrician, dancer, sister of Max, friend to Rowdy and Scruffy, will you and your wonderful entourage do me the honour of accepting my hand in marriage?'

And what was a girl to say to that?

She gazed up at their audience. Every medic in the doctors' house, plus anyone taking refuge there, and there were quite a few, Harry, Luke, Cal, Gina—this whole crazy community was waiting for her answer with seemingly just as much interest as Alistair.

Even Smiley, snarling between his captors, was being made to wait and listen, for there was no way Harry was taking him away before he'd heard her answer.

So she'd better get on with it.

'Yes, my love,' she said, with all the force she could muster, so her voice rang out over the dying wind, carrying around this old doctors' house which had seen so much and had been the hub of so much pain and pleasure.

'Yes, my love,' she said again, and she smiled up at Alistair with all the love in her heart. 'Yes,

I'll marry you. But only if you kiss me. Right here. Right now.'

And who knew what the audience did then? Georgie Turner didn't care.

MEDICAL™

 **Large Print**

Titles for the next six months...

June

CHRISTMAS EVE BABY	Caroline Anderson
LONG-LOST SON: BRAND-NEW FAMILY	Lilian Darcy
THEIR LITTLE CHRISTMAS MIRACLE	Jennifer Taylor
TWINS FOR A CHRISTMAS BRIDE	Josie Metcalfe
THE DOCTOR'S VERY SPECIAL CHRISTMAS	Kate Hardy
A PREGNANT NURSE'S CHRISTMAS WISH	Meredith Webber

July

THE ITALIAN'S NEW-YEAR MARRIAGE WISH	Sarah Morgan
THE DOCTOR'S LONGED-FOR FAMILY	Joanna Neil
THEIR SPECIAL-CARE BABY	Fiona McArthur
THEIR MIRACLE CHILD	Gill Sanderson
SINGLE DAD, NURSE BRIDE	Lynne Marshall
A FAMILY FOR THE CHILDREN'S DOCTOR	Dianne Drake

August

THE DOCTOR'S BRIDE BY SUNRISE	Josie Metcalfe
FOUND: A FATHER FOR HER CHILD	Amy Andrews
A SINGLE DAD AT HEATHERMERE	Abigail Gordon
HER VERY SPECIAL BABY	Lucy Clark
THE HEART SURGEON'S SECRET SON	Janice Lynn
THE SHEIKH SURGEON'S PROPOSAL	Olivia Gates

 MILLS & BOON®

Pure reading pleasure

0508 LP 2P P1 Med

MEDICAL™

Large Print

September

THE SURGEON'S FATHERHOOD SURPRISE Jennifer Taylor
THE ITALIAN SURGEON CLAIMS HIS Alison Roberts
BRIDE
DESERT DOCTOR, SECRET SHEIKH Meredith Webber
A WEDDING IN WARRAGURRA Fiona Lowe
THE FIREFIGHTER AND THE SINGLE MUM Laura Iding
THE NURSE'S LITTLE MIRACLE Molly Evans

October

THE DOCTOR'S ROYAL LOVE-CHILD Kate Hardy
HIS ISLAND BRIDE Marion Lennox
A CONSULTANT BEYOND COMPARE Joanna Neil
THE SURGEON BOSS'S BRIDE Melanie Milburne
A WIFE WORTH WAITING FOR Maggie Kingsley
DESERT PRINCE, EXPECTANT MOTHER Olivia Gates

November

NURSE BRIDE, BAYSIDE WEDDING Gill Sanderson
BILLIONAIRE DOCTOR, ORDINARY Carol Marinelli
NURSE
THE SHEIKH SURGEON'S BABY Meredith Webber
THE OUTBACK DOCTOR'S SURPRISE BRIDE Amy Andrews
A WEDDING AT LIMESTONE COAST Lucy Clark
THE DOCTOR'S MEANT-TO-BE MARRIAGE Janice Lynn

MILLS & BOON®
Pure reading pleasure

0508 LP 2P P2 Medical